PR

If you're looking for high stakes romance, wildland firefighting hotshots, mysteries and danger abounding, all wrapped up in a package of faith and family, look no further. *Firestorm* kept me fully engaged and totally reading it every second I could. I can't get enough of these characters and stories.

MICHAELA, GOODREADS

What a wonderful addition to this series. Phillips crafted an outstanding story with second chances, secrets, danger, tension, cameo appearances, and Easter eggs.

ALLYSON, GOODREADS

Lisa Phillips has created an outstanding new installment to the Chasing Fire: Montana series with *Firestorm*. Readers are engulfed in deeply hidden secrets, a budding romance, a deadly fire, and a crime. Packed with heartfelt emotion, *Firestorm* contained constant action and ever deepening personal dynamics, which created a complex plot sure to capture the senses. One not to be missed!

KATHRYN, GOODREADS

FIRESTORM

CHASING FIRE MONTANA | BOOK 4

A SERIES CREATED BY SUSAN MAY WARREN AND LISA PHILLIPS

LISA PHILLIPS

sunrise
PUBLISHING

Firestorm
Chasing Fire: Montana, Book 4
Copyright © 2024 Sunrise Media Group LLC
Print ISBN: 978-1-963372-15-1
Ebook ISBN: 978-1-963372-14-4

This book is a work of fiction. Names, characters, places, and
incidents are either products of the author's imagination or used
fictitiously. Any similarity to actual people, organizations, and/or
events is purely coincidental.

All Scripture quotations, unless otherwise indicated, are taken from
the King James Version.

For more information about Lisa Phillips, please access the author's
website at www.authorlisaphillips.com.

Published in the United States of America.
Cover Design: Lynnette Bonner

For me, be it Christ, be it Christ hence to live:
If Jordan above me shall roll,
No pang shall be mine, for in death as in life
Thou wilt whisper Thy peace to my soul.

ONE

Everything was going according to plan.

Kind of.

Firefighter Charlie Benning stared down the flames, then turned and swung his axe at the tree. If they didn't get this line cut, the fire would jump to the trees on the other side of the deer trail and spread toward residences.

So long as the wind didn't change, they had a shot at containing this fire so it didn't destroy any more of the Kootenai National Forest. In the last week, the blaze had nearly doubled in size. It was spreading north and had split into two forks, with the western tine headed for the town of Snowhaven.

He lifted his axe again.

Pain ripped through his side at his lower back. He hissed and barely managed to keep the axe from flying at one of the other hotshots on this team.

"Whoa." Kane, one of the "Trouble Boys" as they'd been dubbed by the others, grabbed the axe handle. "Easy there." The guy had close-shaved dark-blond hair and eyes one of the female hotshots had described as brooding.

Charlie grunted. "I'm good." But he let Kane take the axe. That guy's broody eyes saw way too much, and Charlie had been avoiding anything personal since the fire season started.

It wasn't time to slip up now. Not when the fire had grown big enough that his plan had a shot at working. The alternative would be messy. This had to go one way.

"Why don't you take a water break?" Kane turned and hammered at the tree with more strength than Charlie had even back when he was in his twenties. He was over the hill of four and zero now—a fact the hotshots insisted on reminding him of every day, calling him "old man" and "grandpa."

Might've bothered him before, but not lately.

Charlie walked off the pain as he headed for the water barrel Hammer had carried out here. The fellow hotshot went by Ham most of the time, and he saw way too much with that military situational awareness he wore like a coat.

Everyone knew walking something off didn't work. Not when the doctor had used words like *chronic* and *dialysis*.

He'd left Last Chance County before that conversation could turn to *stage two* or *failure*. Then he'd fudged the medical part of acceptance onto the hotshot crew—bypassing rookie training with the courses he'd taken over the years as a firefighter. He knew what he was doing. The truth would come out eventually, but that would be after the fact.

Too late.

Charlie might have had a decorated career in rescue squad, but he also had a failed marriage and an estranged daughter he'd dropped off at the teen

2

firefighter camp up in the mountains. Wildlands Academy would be her home for the summer, and at the end of the season, Charlie would have done what he needed to do.

Everything would be taken care of.

Charlie patted the letter in his bulky fire-pants pocket, tucked next to the shelter he was supposed to never have to deploy.

"You good?" The boss lifted his chin. Conner Young was a good man, a family guy like Charlie would never be.

He lifted his chin in reply. "Probably just pulled a muscle." He got a drink, wishing for a moment of solitude he could use to take a pill, and turned to watch the hotshot crew.

Two women, seven men, not including him. The two youngest guys were in their early twenties— which made him old enough to be their father.

A thought that didn't make him feel more spry.

"I checked the weather report this morning. If that front comes over from the coast like they think, the fire could change directions and head to the firefighter camp, Wildlands Academy." Charlie pulled a map from his pants pocket and unfolded it.

Conner nodded. "I'm waiting for Miles to confirm, but I think we'll get redeployed after this to head up there."

Charlie marked the path of the wind. If it came in from the west, it could funnel through a valley that would lead right to the camp north of them.

Orion Price lowered his Pulaski and headed over. The guy was twenty-two but had more experience as a hotshot than most of the crew. The kid had gel in his dark-blond hair and features that were familiar even though Charlie had never met him before this summer.

Now that he knew who Orion's mother was, it made sense.

The guy said, "Not sure we need to worry about the academy. They'll be protected even if the fire heads in that direction. It was designed that way, and Mom keeps the vegetation cut back."

"Yeah?" Charlie liked the kid. Not too much of a know-it-all, and not so quiet like the youngest hotshot, Mack, that he never said a word.

Conner said, "Jayne knows what she's doing."

Her name cut through him like someone had taken their Pulaski and hammered it into him. Didn't matter that he knew she lived there and ran Wildlands Academy now. She hadn't been there the day he'd dropped off his daughter Alexis. That was the way he'd designed it. Purposely, so he didn't run into Jayne.

Jayne Price, the girl he'd loved at seventeen and walked away from—never looking back. Orion's mother. The woman who ran the teen firefighter camp. He would never *not* react to her.

And whatever odd expression was on his face hadn't gone unnoticed. *Quit thinking about her.*

Orion frowned at him. "She's been working at the camp since before I was born. It's a fire safety camp. The whole place was designed to keep from catching fire, even if it's completely surrounded by flames. The trees are at least thirty feet back from the cabins and the main house. There's a lake to the west, so they can get a quick water drop if necessary."

Charlie managed to nod. "And your dad?" He hadn't asked yet. As if he wanted to know that she was happily married now. Or that Orion loved his dad in a way Alexis would never feel about him. Charlie shook off the thoughts. He was the one who'd walked away from her at the end of the summer and gone home to Last Chance County. He hoped she had been happy all these years.

Orion shrugged. "Don't have one. Never have."

Oof. Sore subject much? Charlie didn't need to care about Jayne's love life—which was apparently as good as his had been in the twenty years since they'd seen each other. The thing he'd had with Alexis's mother had been a bad idea from start to finish. They'd both made it worse, and Alexis had suffered in the middle. So Charlie had opted to make himself scarce versus making it harder for his daughter with all the friction between him and her mother.

Charlie said, "I dropped off my daughter Alexis at the camp at the beginning of summer. I'm going to worry."

"Have you called her, asked her what they can see of the fire?"

He tried not to stiffen at Conner's question, just saying, "Uh, no. Haven't been able to get through. Ry, what about your mom? Have you checked in with her recently?"

The son of the woman he had never quit thinking about blinked. "I...uh." Orion cleared his throat. "We had a fight. Right at the beginning of the season. She doesn't even know I broke up with Laina over Memorial Day weekend."

Conner set a hand on Orion's shoulder. "You haven't spoken to her at all?"

The kid shrugged it off. "She hasn't called me either."

Charlie wanted to tell the guy to suck it up and make amends, but that would make him the biggest hypocrite west of Denver. He'd sent Alexis two texts at the beginning of summer, but his seventeen-year-old hadn't replied.

They'd been estranged since before his ex-wife had lost out to her protracted battle with cancer. Now Alexis was grieving the loss of her mother, and he had to figure out how to get her to let him be her father with the time he had left.

He didn't know how to fix that. But he could fix the rest of it.

If he got everything to go as planned.

"Whoa." One of the guys yelled from behind them, about fifteen feet away.

"Houston!" That was Emily who'd screamed.

Charlie turned to watch her scramble back, falling as she moved away from what had everyone's attention. Houston had vanished into the earth in the center of a circle of hotshots. A cave-in, or some kind of sink hole?

Hammer got down on his stomach and inched forward. The ground in front of him caved in, and the whole area rumbled under them. Charlie got closer to the hole, grabbing Mack's arm when he started toward his brother. "Don't become another victim." To the group he said, "Everyone take a step back. Ham, stay where you are."

"I can see him." The guy was military. It wasn't something a guy like Ham could hide. His history of service was there in the way he walked, the way he focused right now.

Kane and Saxon, his buddies, hid it better. Mack appeared to be along for the ride as Ham's kid brother. They regularly orbited Sanchez—the female hotshot—in a way that looked an awful lot like they were a protective detail.

They certainly had secrets. Maybe one day the world would discover what they were, but it wouldn't be today.

"Stay where you are." Charlie knelt by Ham's feet and tried to see into the hole Houston had fallen into. All he saw was the top of Houston's bald head and the nasty burn scars he had on one side of his face. Charlie called out, "Hey, Pastor! You good?"

No reply.

He patted Ham's leg. "Tell me what you can see."

"Shoulder. Side of his head." Where those burn scars were. "No blood. But he's pretty buried. It's covering his chest and lower body. Not sure if he's breathing."

"He's not too far down." Charlie turned to the group. "Rope. We need to rappel in and pull him out."

"Whoever goes down will end up being buried with dirt like Houston." Orion pulled on his gloves. "Then we'll have two victims."

Charlie said, "That's why we're going to hook in and use a pulley system to get them both out. Houston, and whoever goes down after him."

Saxon stared at the hole with his dark gaze and those Middle Eastern features. "Looks like a tunnel down there."

Orion huffed. "I suppose you want to be the hero, Charlie?"

So everyone could realize he wasn't able to do the things he'd done every day with rescue squad in Last Chance County? Nope. "You want this, Ry?"

Orion nodded.

"Then hook up. We need to get Houston out before more dirt piles on him and we have to call Sophie and tell her we lost him."

Conner gave Charlie a dark look. Charlie ignored it and got to work, organizing everyone so there were guys holding the rope as Orion went in. He had the kid tie another loop around Houston, under his arms. Team two pulled Houston while team one pulled out Orion.

"Let me see him." Charlie knelt beside Houston and tugged off one glove. He felt for a pulse, then checked Houston's breathing. He patted his friend's cheek. "Don't make me call home and tell the chief his brother fell through a hole in the ground."

Houston pulled in a breath and coughed. Dirt expelled from between his lips.

Charlie let out a breath. "There you are."

"Don't tell Macon."

Charlie chuckled. "That goes both ways, brother."

"Deal." Houston sat up, groaning.

Conner said, "Charlie, Orion, take Houston back to town in my truck. Get him checked out at the hospital. The rest of us will finish up here and hit the bus. We're getting redeployed to the north edge of the fire so we can cut it off from up there." Then he pointed at the sky.

A series of parachutes dropped from a plane to the north, always a sight to see. The Ember smokejumpers had been sent in, probably to contain the blaze from the north and push back against the edge before it ravaged the entire county.

Charlie picked out his lieutenant, Logan Crawford, in the middle of the line. He heard someone mutter a prayer for their protection.

Conner clapped his gloves together. "Let's move out."

"Let's get that pile cleared away!" Jayne Price pointed at the stack of brush the kids had cleared. This area to the east of a fire road an hour's walk from Wildlands Academy hadn't been cut back in weeks. "Down to the road. Okay, guys?"

"On it." A couple of teen boys, normally eager, walked a lot slower now. The Masterson twins from Benson, whose parents worked search and rescue, had jumped at every challenge she and her staff had presented to them. But it had been a long day.

All in all they had fifteen kids, a mix of male and female. Right now all of them were tired and dirty, probably sick of sucking in the gray air. Most had given up brushing falling ash from their clothes and hair.

They had a couple of guys from town that came out with them on field trips or came up to camp and taught classes. One was a crusty old firefighter who'd fought blazes in the sixties and seventies. The other had been a smokejumper, and the kids always sat riveted, listening to stories of jumping out of planes to fight fire.

They'd all been out here for hours, working like hotshots to slow the spread of a fire that might come this direction.

Thanks to the way God had carved this canyon, the smoke hung above them like a ceiling of cloud. But they wouldn't be able to stay out here much longer when the air quality was so bad. Not without suffering long-term effects—the way her grandpa had. She could hear that wet-rattle cough in her mind even though he'd died when she was much younger than these kids.

She strode down the line, her boots kicking up the dusty earth.

"Doesn't look good." Her administrator walked over to meet her. Bridget Willis had been working at the camp since back when Jayne had been one of these kids—the summer her life had flipped upside down. A story she'd broken down and decided to tell the kids last night over the cooking fire while their dinner hot dogs sizzled. All because two of her campers had been caught sneaking off.

Not unheard of—after all, it was what Jayne had done. Then it was what Logan and one of the camp girls had done years after, and so many others. She'd seen Logan in the grocery store at the beginning of summer, and they'd had a good ole laugh about that.

But it wasn't funny.

Even if she had Orion as a result, she didn't need more parents complaining to her that their kids had spent summer at her camp and learned more than just wildland firefighting. Wildlands Academy was about learning to be a hotshot. Building strength of mind and body—and strength of character.

Bridget, in her fifties and more comfortable in a library, glanced at the smoke to the west. She'd surprised Jayne from the beginning with her brand new hiking boots and a smile that never got tired. "That weather report didn't do it justice. The wind is picking up."

Jayne nodded. "Let's get this brush in the truck and head to the river. They might get up close and personal with the fire tonight, but it won't jump the water."

One of the girls walked by her. Alexis Martin, one of the older teens, had been giving her the cold shoulder all morning. The girl glanced aside at Jayne when she thought Jayne wasn't looking, peering between the strands of the brown curls that fell to her shoulders.

Because of the story Jayne had told them all? Her cautionary tale of why hookups were a bad idea. She had no idea why the seventeen-year-old reacted that way over Jayne's sordid tale of a summer romance and discovering two months later that she was pregnant. She'd kept the tale youth-group friendly, but teens responded better when she was "real" with them, and that meant being honest about why she had a grown son and no husband.

About the boy named Charlie who had swept her into what had felt like a dream.

Bridget clapped her hands together. "Listen up, everyone! We're heading to the river."

More than one teen groaned.

"We know you're tired," Jayne called out. "But the wind is picking up, and if it changes direction, we could end up in trouble."

They were all kitted out in fire gear. They knew what to do in a disaster scenario—each one had a fire shelter. Safety was a nonnegotiable for her.

"I've never lost a firefighter, and I won't break that streak today. So we push to the river, and then we break out the soap and get cleaned up. Who wants my famous spicy gumbo for dinner? Maybe we can do those hot ham and cheese sandwiches tomorrow."

That picked up a few spirits. Thankfully Jayne

11

had set it up in the slow cooker back in the camp lodge before they'd come out this morning, so it should be about ready. They were going to camp out overnight, but that didn't mean not eating well.

They just had to get to a good spot.

She said, "S'mores for dessert."

That got the rest of them moving.

Bridget said, "Let's get this brush to the truck so I can go pick up dinner from camp and bring it out."

"I'll take a pepperoni pizza." One of the guys grinned—Mr. Romance, who'd convinced Shelly from California (not Shelly from Alaska) to sneak off into the bushes with him last night after bed down. Jayne had spotted them more than once, and it was why she'd decided to tell the story.

"I'll get right on that." Bridget grinned.

The crew started grabbing bundles of brush and walking down the trail to the truck they had on hand for emergencies and supply delivery. Other than that, they were alone out here. Carrying what they needed, and walking from camp nearly ten miles to the northwest.

Most years there were a few fires they could help put out by clearing lines hotshots had already dug to keep this area safe, all the while praying the fire stayed far away and even that it might head in another direction entirely.

It didn't look like that prayer would be answered today, so she asked for wisdom instead and protection for the kids—and all the firefighters. Not just her son Orion, but every one of them, and the smokejumpers she'd seen parachute overhead a bit ago.

She wasn't a stranger to unanswered prayers.

God didn't say yes to everything, and why should

12

He when He knew far better than she did? If the wind blew the fire toward them and the camp, then the outcome would be in His hands.

Jayne tugged on the hem of each glove, then picked up a bundle of brush in her arms and raced one of the kids to the truck parked on the fire road a quarter mile to the north.

Alexis dumped her load in the truck bed beside Jayne's.

Jayne caught her attention as they turned. "Everything okay?"

The girl shot her an odd look. "Sure." Alexis brushed hair back from her face and wound up with a smear of dirt on her forehead. "Your son...the one you mentioned. Does he ever come around the camp?"

"Sometimes." Jayne wasn't going to lie to the girl. "We actually had a pretty big fight at the beginning of the fire season." Her stomach clenched and she looked at the thirty-foot pine trees that stood in two rows flanking the fire road. "He wants to be a smokejumper. That's...it's actually what killed my dad. His parachute failed."

Alexis studied her, entirely too much pain in her eyes. She'd suffered loss, but for the most part refused to talk about it.

"Who did you lose?"

Alexis said, "My mom died right after Christmas. Couple days before New Year. She had cancer."

"I'm sorry for your loss."

The girl winced. "It was..." She shrugged. "I don't even know. It was bad for a long time. But she wasn't a nice person, which sounds like a horrible thing to say about someone who's dead."

13

"All we can do is be honest about how we feel." Jayne set a hand on the girl's shoulder. "God knows it before we even come to Him, but He wants us to talk to Him. To build that relationship and rely on Him for our comfort and strength. It sounds hard, but it's actually very simple."

Jayne had no idea where the girl was with faith. She made no secret of the way she guided the kids. If they needed help or advice, it was going to be based on the Bible—the book Jayne had lived her life by since Orion was born and she'd realized he needed more than she could give him.

The teen shook her head. "There's nothing simple about this."

Alexis had said her father had custody of her and that he was a hotshot in Ember for the summer. With the exception of the time since yesterday, when she'd told her teenage love story, Alexis had been her right-hand girl so far this summer. In a lot of ways, she'd come to rely on the teen, who had some basic medical training and a lifeguard certification and was planning on getting an EMT certificate next year in her senior year of high school. The girl was going to make something of her life, even if none of the adults she had watching out for her had ever encouraged her to do it.

Alexis was going places, and she didn't need anyone's help. Maybe it was worry for her father that had Alexis out of sorts. If she were Jayne's daughter, Jayne would be proud of the way she carried on after her mother passed and her father dumped her here for the summer so he could join the Jude County Hotshots. The way she was proud of Orion and the good he was doing in the world every day, not just during fire season. Her son had grown up to be a good man.

Despite who his father was.

"I'm gonna go help with the rest." Alexis wandered off toward the brush that still needed clearing.

Jayne checked on everyone and kept one eye on the clouds in the distance as she did it, then she looked at her phone to see if there were any new updates.

It chimed as she pulled it from her belt holster, and she sucked in a breath. *It's worse than I thought.* The text from Miles and the update from the National Interagency Fire Center in Idaho was a double alert—and they needed to respond in double time.

"Hustle up, everyone! Change of dinner plans. The camp has been upgraded to 'Ready to go' status. We need to get back there and be prepared to evacuate."

TWO

"WE HAVE A BAY NEXT DOOR." THE NURSE WAVED at the wall. "We can get you checked out as well. The doctor will be free soon."

Charlie froze. Standing at the end of the bed had been a bad choice. He should've had Orion come in here with Houston while Charlie checked in with their incident commander.

Houston's half an eyebrow rose. He had a scratch down the side of his face and neck, abrasions on his arms, and a split lip.

Charlie looked at the nurse. "I'm not the one who fell in a hole in the ground."

Houston snorted. "You called Sophie, right?"

Charlie nodded. "She's on her way." He'd had to talk her through the initial panic and reassure her that Houston might be grazed and a bit banged up, but mostly it was just a ploy to get back to town so he could see her, even if it was because she was visiting him at the hospital. She'd laughed, and he'd known then she was good to drive herself.

The nurse eyed him. "You sure you're good, Hotshot?"

Charlie said, "I've got it handled."

She left the room.

"You've got what handled?" Houston lay back in the bed, his hotshot clothes getting dirt all over the sheets. "Don't worry. No one else noticed, I don't think."

"How did you?" Charlie gripped the rail at the end of the bed.

"I'm a little more people focused than most. You aren't okay, Charlie."

Unsurprising he'd figured this out, considering Houston had been a pastor before this summer of firefighting and he would probably return to that vocation right after.

"What is it?" Houston asked.

Charlie ducked his head, hardly wanting to say the words *kidney disease*. He looked up. "Like I said, I've got it handled."

Houston studied him for a moment. "I'm around. If you wanna talk about it."

Charlie shook his hand. "Thanks."

Houston's brother had been Charlie's fire chief in Last Chance County. Between Logan—a smokejumper for the summer season—and Houston, and a more recent transplant, Dakota Masterson, there was entirely too much of home here. He'd tried to escape somewhere no one would care. That had hardly happened when he had people here who definitely did.

But when the alternative was to push everyone away, what was he supposed to do?

"Don't worry about me." Charlie headed for the exit and found Orion on the sidewalk, pacing, phone to his ear. Over the mountains in the distance, he could see the plume of wildfire smoke, but all he could smell were the lavender bushes in planters on either side of the automatic doors.

"Copy that, Commander." Orion turned sideways and Charlie got a look at his profile.

It never failed to hit him how much the young man favored his mother in the line of his nose and his blue eyes. But there was something else in the kid. Something his father had given him that Charlie couldn't let go of.

Orion said, "We'll head there now."

Charlie lifted his hand to shield his eyes from the afternoon sun.

Orion hung up the phone. "We're going to the camp so we can help evacuate if it comes to that. Miles has been trying to reach my mom on the camp phone, but there's no answer."

"Did you try her cell?"

Orion nodded. "If they're out on a hike, there are spots where there's no signal. Could be they're just in a dead zone."

"All right." Charlie handed over the keys.

Much as he'd like to have occupied himself with the task of driving Conner's truck, he needed to rest, or his body would shut down for the day.

It would take the better part of an hour to get to the camp. Charlie buckled up and put his head back. "Wanna tell me what's up between you and your mom?"

The kid was a good firefighter. He loved the job as much as he loved this land, something Charlie couldn't say about any piece of geography on the map.

That camp was the closest Charlie had come to

18

loving anything until the day Alexis had grabbed ahold of his heart. The minute she'd wrapped her tiny newborn hand around his finger, he was a goner. And from that moment on, Helena had used their child as a weapon against him.

When it became clear how it affected Alexis to be in the middle like that, he'd filed for divorce.

Helena had driven a wedge between them.

Orion looked over. "Do you want to talk about you and Alexis and how you dropped your kid off at camp and haven't talked to her since?"

Charlie stared out the window. They drove past Hot Cakes Bakery. Farther through town, the Hotline, a local bar and grill, had a nearly full parking lot even though it was still early evening. The favorite hangout of hotshots and smokejumpers and all their support personnel, and groupies he had no interest in.

"That's what I thought."

Charlie didn't want to leave it like that. Maybe someone should hear it from him, since he hadn't ever told anyone at the Eastside Firehouse what the deal was with his personal life.

"It's complicated." Charlie let out a long breath. "My ex? We got divorced before Alexis turned six. I barely saw my daughter after that, even though I was supposed to have alternating weekends."

He saw Orion glance over.

"Helena used my firefighter schedule as a weapon. Said a child needed more stability." Charlie squeezed his knees. "Alexis was nine when the neighbor called 911 because the stove was on fire. Helena had been out for more than a day, and Alexis was making herself dinner, but it'd spilled over and caught fire."

19

"Did you get custody after that?" Orion's voice had softened.

"The judge was her boyfriend's father. He ruled in her favor. I got even less allotted time with her than I'd had before. I found whatever ways I could to see her. Volunteering at her school on my days off, working as a janitor. Showing her how she could ride her bike to the firehouse in the summer, when her mom was at work." Charlie shook his head. "Her mom had all that time to get in her head. Alexis would say things, and it was Helena's words that came out of her mouth."

"So she poisoned her against you."

"Her points weren't without merit." Charlie shifted far enough to dig in his pocket. "I had bad periods. Seasons where I figured, what was the point? If that's what she wanted to tell everyone, then why bother trying to prove her wrong when no one believed it." He held up the chip. "Six years sober."

"Wow. Congratulations."

Charlie tucked it away. "Why did you want to be a firefighter?"

"My grandpa was a smokejumper. Mom doesn't like to talk about it, but I read the reports. It was a tragic accident." He gripped the wheel with both hands. "I grew up at the camp. By the time I was twelve, I knew there was nothing else I wanted to do."

"Me too." Charlie hadn't found value in anything else. "My dad was a Vietnam vet. Cranky drunk, and a violent one. My grandpa, World War II, but with less booze and more Jesus. He took me to church while my dad slept off his Saturday night benders."

Orion took a turn off the highway. It should've looked familiar to Charlie, but it had been too long.

Would Jayne look familiar?

He glanced at Orion.

The kid said, "That was quick thinking, with Houston."

Charlie shrugged. "Ten years on rescue squad."

"And you never wanted to be a lieutenant?"

"They don't promote guys like me."

"Why come here for the summer?" Orion slowed as the asphalt turned to packed-down dirt and gravel.

Vegetation on the sides of the road had been cleared. The long, dry spring had bowed to a hot summer. They needed rain, but the forecast was nothing but hot winds and clear skies.

He spotted something between the trees. People, or deer. Whoever—or whatever—it was, they were gone nearly as fast as they'd come.

Charlie said, "Montana seemed like a good place to be."

Orion pulled into the camp, under the wood beam with WILDLANDS ACADEMY carved into it. A huge lodge to the left, three cabins to the right. Barns and outbuildings. Even a tire swing.

Years fell away, and he could see her in his mind. Feel her blonde hair between his fingers. He could almost taste her smile.

You're going to get me in trouble, Benning.

And he had. The two of them had nearly been kicked out of camp.

"Let's check the lodge." Orion shoved the car in Park. "If they're out, it should be on the schedule."

Charlie followed him through the door into the alcove. "Smells the same."

Orion glanced over. "You've been here?"

Charlie found the wall of photos and walked along until he found the right year. He tapped the photo with his index finger. "Summer before senior year."

"That was the year my mom was here." Orion frowned.

Charlie turned to him. "I knew her."

Orion said, "We don't have time for memory lane. We need to find them so we can make sure they're safe. You felt the winds changing."

He had. "Where are they?"

Orion showed him the map on the wall. "We should take ATVs, or we'll be hiking for hours. You don't look like you've got ten miles in you. You look like you need a nap, old man." The kid clapped him on the shoulder. "I'll grab some food so we can get your energy up."

Charlie said, "I'm not hungry," and headed for the door.

"Don't leave without me."

His grip snagged the door handle, and he turned to look at Orion's retreating back. "Doesn't matter what I do, kid. This fire will blow up anyway."

And he wasn't talking about the one in the forest.

He'd tried to avoid coming to Wildlands Academy when she was there, and now he was going to run into Jayne whether he wanted to or not. No way that wouldn't end in an inferno of anger and hurt feelings over the way he'd left it years ago—and what he wanted from her now. He might know how to put out a blaze of heat and destruction. That was his job.

But this was personal.

22

The singing had died down several minutes ago, and Jayne hadn't started a new song. She wanted to sing "It Is Well," the hymn she had held dear to her heart for years, but an upbeat song proved more effective at lifting spirits over a long hike.

Alexis trailed behind her, not saying anything. Bridget led the group, and Jayne brought up the rear as they hiked the deer trail back to camp. She kept glancing back but didn't know what to say to Alexis. She should be focusing on keeping the kids safe right now rather than the emotional state of one teen.

The orange sun hung low in the hazy afternoon sky. Warm wind whipped at the strands that had come loose from her ponytail.

Jayne might have raised a boy, but she'd mentored enough teen girls to know that whatever was going on might blow over by the time they got back to camp. Alexis could bounce back to engaged and willing to participate rather than the standoffish teen behind Jayne right now. She had to draw a line between instructor and friend on occasion—like when she'd told them the story of herself and Charlie last night.

Usually she didn't mention his name, and she had no idea why it'd slipped out. Even Orion didn't know his father's name. She'd never given it to him, and he'd never asked—though she'd offered to tell him whatever he wanted to know. He'd told her that he hadn't needed a father growing up and didn't need one now that he was an adult.

Cue heartbreak.

He had mentors and father figures of his own. But the dream of a family had never died, even if her life indicated that it wouldn't happen.

A girl in front of her, Shelly from Alaska, glanced back. She'd been in a pretty intense conversation with Aria, who knew Alexis from Last Chance County, but now said, "Do you think we'll need to evacuate the camp?"

"It's possible. I'll know the moment they upgrade us to evacuation status, and there's plenty to do with the time until then."

Shelly slowed so she could walk beside Jayne. "Has the camp ever burned down before?"

"A long time ago." The year Orion turned seven. "Since then, we've reconfigured a lot of things and made it as hard as possible for any fire in the area to reach the structures."

It meant the space around the buildings had little shade from trees, but the tradeoff was that fire had nothing to jump to between the trees and the buildings—all of which had metal roofs.

"My dad is a hotshot for the team where I live in Alaska. Their whole headquarters burned down last year, so the firefighters set up camp in the field behind our house." She grinned. "I made coffee all day and all night for, like, three weeks until they'd suppressed the fire enough to start rebuilding."

Jayne said, "A lot of people think they have to do big things in order to make a difference in the world. Sometimes it's small things, like making coffee for a group of firefighters, that keeps everything running."

Alexis snorted behind her. "The firehouse where my dad works always smells like coffee. But it never tastes any good. More like it's been sitting there too long."

"You hang out there when he's working?" She hadn't said much about her dad, who had dropped her off at camp the morning Jayne was in town picking up the groceries. She'd said more about her mom's tough battle with cancer, though she'd cut off the conversation as soon as they got close to the grief.

Jayne didn't know who Alexis Martin's father was, but the girl acted a whole lot like she had no one in her life to support her. She'd like to chat with the guy when he picked her up at the end of summer. Maybe even give him a piece of her mind.

Jayne's phone started to buzz in her pocket. "Looks like we've got our signal back." Much of the area had no cell signal, but this ridge got them within the tower's coverage. She pulled it out—and so did every single teen on the trail. "Don't trip 'cause you're staring at your phone."

Her notifications loaded. Missed calls. Text messages from Orion. A weather update from NIFC—the National Interagency Fire Center headquartered in Boise. Notifications from the BLM and the Ember Incident Commander.

She looked at the ones from Orion first.

ORION

Fire headed to camp. On our way.

Then another:

Saw you're up at the river today.
Headed to you on ATVs.

He was coming here?

She could text back, but if he was driving one of the ATVs they kept at camp, she didn't need to distract him.

She went into her maps app and shared her

location with him, just so he would get an accurate update while she had connection.

"Lake!"

The shout came from the front of the line so the kids would know they were in sight of the lake.

Immediately the line started moving faster. A couple of kids—the twins, Samuel and Joshua Masterson, whose parents were on a search and rescue team based out of Benson, Washington, where they lived—raced to the lake with another boy, Tiger Christiansen, and they all waded in fully clothed so they could cool off.

Others stood by the bank so the ones in the water could splash them. Mostly it turned into the boys flinging handfuls of water and the girls squealing.

Jayne stuck to the dirt path between the storage sheds and the rocky shore, smiling at their antics. They kept the kayaks locked up most of the time but took them out often to let the kids take a break from training to blow off steam. They all had work to do at the camp, but she never begrudged them a second to cool off. They'd worked hard today.

One of the boys pulled himself up onto the floating dock at least a quarter mile toward the middle of the lake and pumped his arms in the air. He did a backflip off the dock back into the water in full view of the girls.

Jayne dropped her pack and leaned against the shed in the shade, doing a quick head count of teens and staff.

The camp was another mile down the trail, which most of the boys would run in their wet socks, carrying their boots so they didn't get damp.

Her phone buzzed with a text.

ORION

> You're closer than I thought. Doubling back.

She scanned around the lake.

A helicopter crested the mountain on the far side of the lake, carrying a water container. It flew low, left to right, behind her designated swim area, and picked up water.

The kids on the bank, and the two on the dock now, all cheered as the helicopter lifted up and headed to dump the water on fire nearby.

Jayne waved.

She spotted movement on the opposite edge of the lake, where a trail snaked around the bank in the trees.

Moving fast, like an ATV—two of them.

She kept scanning and didn't see movement at the cabins she rented out—no sign of the mysterious resident who had shown up a few weeks ago with barely an explanation as to why he couldn't have booked online. She'd thought about contacting the sheriff, but the guy seemed exhausted more than anything else. He'd left the camp alone and they'd reciprocated.

Though, she had sent a copy of his driver's license to the sheriff. Hutchinson hadn't called her back with any issues on the guy's name.

An ATV emerged from the trees. Orion. Behind him, another firefighter drove the second ATV.

She pushed off the shed but didn't go far out of the shade as they headed toward her down the trail. Alexis turned from the group she stood with and strode over for some reason.

Jayne lifted her hand and quietly thanked God for the chance to speak with her son after so much silence.

She got a look at the man behind him, and her legs nearly gave out. She stumbled back a step. Dark-brown hair that needed cutting, a day or two of beard growth that made him look grizzly. Those shoulders he'd had at seventeen were broader now, even if he was slender.

No. Why was he here? That uniform. He filled it out like a man comfortable with who he was. Charlie Benning was a hotshot with Orion. They had to have been working together all summer. Did that mean he knew…

Alexis came to stand beside Jayne. "I guess you're surprised to see him. The boyfriend from your cautionary tale."

Jayne choked on a whimper. *Charlie.*

"Mom?" Orion hopped off the ATV.

Charlie killed the engine on his and did the same, still lean and muscled like he had been at seventeen. But where the boy she'd known used to be, now there was a man.

She put her hand on her front. He was really here, and after she'd spent years wishing he would show back up. Wishing she could tell him. *Lord…* Did she have the right to ask for help?

"Dad?" Alexis stared as he walked over. "Why are you…how much weight have you lost since fire season started?"

He didn't answer her. He stared at Jayne, and she surveyed his dark hair, threads of silver on his temples. The lines of decades of firefighting on his face. The shadow of loss she knew well. *My mom died right after Christmas.* She stared at him, knowing what he saw. She was dirty from the hike, covered in ash, her hair braided back and probably all disheveled by now. Old boots and worn hands.

"Okay, so this is Charlie's daughter. What else is going on? Mom, you okay?"

Orion's question jerked her attention around. "Ry…"

Before Jayne could say anything else, Alexis did. "We should probably talk."

Orion glanced at her, giving a tight shake of his head. "Why is that?"

Alexis set a hand on her hip. "Because I think you're my brother. The son of Jayne and the boyfriend in her *cautionary tale.* My dad."

Her son turned around to her. The man who was once the boy who had torn her heart to shreds did the same. Charlie looked at Orion, and then back at her, a kind of wonder on his face mixed with anger. A sick feeling roiled in her stomach.

Charlie said, "Jayne."

"Mom." Orion's face reddened. His hands balled into fists by his sides. "Is she right? Is…is Charlie my father?"

She could see the matched expressions on their faces. *You never told me.*

Jayne's stomach clenched. "Yes. Charlie is your father."

She looked from him to the man beside him. "Charlie, this is your son."

THREE

CHARLIE BLINKED AGAINST THE RED HAZE OF ANGER he'd tried for years to tamp down when it threatened to overtake him.

An older woman headed toward them, looking at each one in turn before she said to Jayne, "The propane delivery will be here soon. I'll take the kids."

Jayne nodded, her face pale. This older, more mature version of the girl he'd loved was still stunning. No less than she had been at seventeen. Blonde hair, blue eyes. A smile that had made his knees weak. Hands he'd held, fingers he'd stared at, wondering how they could be so strong and so soft.

Charlie looked at his daughter, aware of his son's attention as well, but he had to know if she was all right. He tried to communicate that with his expression.

How much weight have you lost?

She knew. It wasn't surprising, considering how astute she was. And the question hadn't been concern so much as an accusation. Maybe there was care underneath somewhere...

Deep underneath.

But the bottom line was the thing he'd been avoiding since the beginning of summer. She knew now that he wasn't okay. He *hadn't* hidden it from her.

The older woman cupped her hands around her mouth. "Let's go, everyone! Back to camp!"

Jayne called out, "Thanks, Bridget!"

Kids started toward the trail behind Alexis, which led to the camp. A couple waded out of the lake. Overhead, a tanker plane flew past, too high to read which one it was.

Bridget turned back. "Alexis, do you want to come with us?" She spoke as though she hadn't noticed the tension between the four of them, standing off against each other. Then her gaze flitted from one to the other, and he realized she knew there was something very wrong.

Charlie looked from his daughter, who had figured this whole thing out first, to Jayne, who'd lied to all of them. Orion was more of a victim, like Charlie. Lied to. Anger spilled from his lips with the words as Charlie said, "Or you can stay here, with *your family*."

Jayne flinched.

Orion glanced at him. "Did you know?"

Alexis was the one who said, "He didn't know."

She looked about as mad as he felt. "Lexi—"

"He had no idea."

She hadn't said that because she cared. More like she was capitalizing on an opportunity to make him look clueless—a shadow of what her mom had taught her.

Alexis walked away, catching up to the other teens.

Orion probably wanted to go as well.

Jayne squeezed the bridge of her nose. "That's

31

why she's been so standoffish since I told that story."
She dropped her hand back to her side. "I messed up.
I told the kids your name." She shook her head. "I
never do that. She must have put it together."

"And you?" Orion turned to face Charlie. "We've
been working together for weeks."

Charlie had wrongly assumed Jayne started a
relationship with someone quickly after the end of
that summer, too busy trying to fix his other
problems. "I didn't see what was right in front of my
face." And he'd wasted time he could've used to get to
know his son.

Time he would never get back.

He looked at his son now. "She never told me she
was pregnant."

Jayne said, "*She* is standing right here."

Orion turned to her. "You lied to both of us."

"I asked if you wanted to know."

Orion looked like he wanted to say something
else, then he turned and just walked away, following
the others who were out of sight now.

Charlie stared at his son's back. Then he looked at
her. He could hardly believe what he'd heard, so
much that he had to ask again.

"He's really my boy?" Fire burned in his gut that
had nothing to do with the land around them. "You
were pregnant when I left?"

Tears spilled from her eyes. "I didn't realize until
two months later."

"And you didn't find me." Never told him. Never
called or wrote a letter or email. Not once. "So I had
no idea that when I met Orion Price, I was coming
face-to-face with my son."

32

She winced and more tears came. "I'm sorry. Is that what you want to hear?"

"You're unbelievable."

"You think it would've been better?" she said. "That you'd have stuck around and been the man we needed you to be?"

"You never gave me the chance." He turned away, reeling so much that the world spun around him. Pain sparked in his lower back. He took a couple of steps so he could sit on the ATV, but he'd moved farther from it than he thought.

She'd made the choice for him, regardless of whether he'd have been able to settle down at that age. Be a father. Maybe a husband, as well. He'd never know if he'd have had it in him back then to do the right thing.

"Charlie—"

His foot snagged on the ground, and he stumbled but didn't go down. He slammed a hand down on the ATV Orion had ridden and caught himself on the metal over the engine. *Hot.* He pulled his hand back and grabbed the handle instead. He shifted and got his behind on the seat, sideways. But that put her in front of him while he leaned against the ATV.

"Are you okay?" Jayne frowned, swiping at her damp cheeks.

"I'm fine." The refrain popped from his mouth, like he'd trained the response on repeat all summer. And even before then, back at the Eastside Firehouse. Trying to convince everyone he was fine, despite the doctor's report. He'd kept the news from the department and cut out before it came to light.

Jayne jogged to a pack leaning against a shed. She

came back with two bottles of water and handed one over.

He chugged the entire thing, trying to figure out when he'd eaten last. Lightheaded and hot from exhaustion and fighting fires. Anyone would understand his need to rest. Didn't mean anything.

Certainly wouldn't cause a person to jump to the truth as a conclusion.

Not before the aftermath of his plan.

Jayne took a sip of hers. "We should take the ATVs back to camp."

He studied her. This stranger he didn't know, and the upset on her face. She should be upset, considering what she'd done. He lowered the bottle. "You didn't think I needed to know?"

Fresh tears sparked in her eyes. "It wasn't...when I found out, it was bad." She winced. "My mom screamed at me and kicked me out."

He knew her father had died when she was a kid, then her grandpa. She'd been at the camp the summer before her senior year, even though her mom told her she would disown Jayne over it. She'd told him that she only wanted to feel close to her dad while she could. Not to actually fight a fire.

Her mom hadn't understood that.

Why was he remembering all this now? It had been twenty years. Twenty-two considering the age of his son. Nearly twenty-three.

Charlie shut his eyes. He needed to take a breath or he'd let out all this anger. Even if he wanted to, what would it change? What was done had been done, and they couldn't go back and change it now. He could spend the rest of the summer with his son.

"I had nothing." She sniffed back tears. "The

camp director saw me on the side of the road, hitchhiking. He picked me up and then let me stay here over the winter. I helped out. After Orion…I never left. I found a home here."

"And you couldn't have called?" He knew she was the director now, but back then he'd have tried, at least, to be there for her. He knew that much.

"I didn't want to get the same treatment my mom gave me." She brushed blonde flyaway strands from her face. Still as beautiful as she'd ever been. Wise. Caring. Smart. The kind of person who'd complete the task and help the person beside her at the same time. "I couldn't take the risk you wouldn't want anything to do with us. It was the hardest decision I've ever made, and I second-guess myself sometimes. But the bottom line is that neither of us were ready for marriage."

"So you raised him alone."

"I had a family here." She motioned in the direction of the camp. "You got married…and had Alexis."

He looked down…at the pocket where he'd tucked the letter he'd written to Jayne. The past and the present, colliding. "You're right. I did do that." Charlie got up and went to the other ATV. "Let's go."

He tucked the bottle in his pocket and drove away from her.

She was going to ruin his entire plan.

Jayne parked the ATV under the carport, behind the other ATV. She used the side door, figuring she knew where Orion had gone. She didn't want to talk to

Charlie. Not after he'd jumped on the other ATV and left her there. Speeding off, spraying dust behind him so that she had to tie a handkerchief around the bottom half of her face. She didn't need to breathe it in.

She tugged the handkerchief down and used the back hall to get to her office. A hundred things rolled through her head. Thoughts about Charlie— and the anger that had been clear on his face. Orion. Alexis. The fire heading toward them. The campers, and the occupant in one of her three rental cabins.

Bridget had taken over management of the teens. When Jayne drove her ATV past the sheds, Bridget had them all gathered around so she could give them instructions.

Ready to leave meant exactly that. She'd have them pack but leave their things in their rooms.

The door to her office was ajar.

Orion sat behind her desk, working on her computer. The camp dog, Sparky, a mutt who'd wandered in one day and bonded to her son, lay beside the desk.

"Did you see anyone in the woods when you and Charlie were looking for me?" Oh, saying his name actually hurt.

Orion didn't look over from the computer monitor. "Is that really what you want to talk about?"

"If there are people in the woods, we'll need to include them if we get an evacuation order." She tossed her gloves on the sideboard, the surface cluttered because she had no junk drawer. Or at least, that was what she always told herself. On the wall, she had a map of the Kootenai ranges, the northeastern edge of Idaho, and the border into Canada.

So much of it was ablaze right now. A couple of fires had met up and morphed into bigger conflagrations.

She might be serving dinner here tonight, or she might be driving the bus full of kids and their things back to town.

"So we're avoiding talking about him?" Orion sat back in the chair.

No news to report, apparently. She'd learned a long time ago that if he had nothing useful to say, then he kept quiet. As though using too many words would be inefficient. He'd always kept his thoughts to himself.

Kind of like Charlie. But without the destructive behavior that had been his trademark back then. At the time it had been a risk, an excitement. When she'd discovered she was pregnant, part of Jayne hadn't wanted to bring all that into the life of an innocent baby.

But what good had it done Orion to not know his father?

"You never asked," she said. "But I also didn't tell you. And that will always be on me."

He gave her a tiny nod. They hadn't parted on good terms, but they'd always been honest with each other. "I can't believe I've been with him this whole summer."

Jayne bit her lip. "What is he like?"

Orion flinched. "Why are you asking me?"

"Alexis has mentioned her father, and her mother—she's deceased."

"So you've got a shot at getting back in there.

37

Mothering another kid like you do with all the ones here."

"Orion Charles Price—" She realized what she'd said.

Right about the time Orion realized what she'd done. "You gave me his name."

Jayne paced back to the sideboard. She set both palms on the edge and hung her head. *Lord, I didn't want it to happen like this.* She'd expected it to never happen. They'd live their own lives and never meet.

Why had he come here, of all places, and done it now, of all the times he could have?

Charlie and Orion would both need to get back to their team of hotshots. Alexis could sure use time with her father so she could settle her grief and begin to heal. Would he be the kind of dad to support her?

Jayne didn't know what quality fatherhood looked like. She certainly knew what it was like to have a mother she never seemed to measure up to. So she'd been honest with Orion about her failures. All the myriad of ways she needed Jesus so badly.

She'd raised a good man who wanted to make his way in the world. As a *smokejumper*. The idea of it made her sweat with fear. "I freaked out at you the last time we talked."

"Are you going to apologize for everything in one day? Tell me how sorry you are for every scraped knee or time I was picked on at school?"

"These are a bit bigger than that." Jayne turned and leaned on the edge of the sideboard. "I should have told him about you."

"I like the way my life turned out." Orion studied her. "How many people can say that?"

"Not many do." She'd tried not to have any

regrets, jumping on spontaneous trips with Orion—a couple that took them past Last Chance County where she knew Charlie had been. "But how can you?"

"You might regret not telling me, but I didn't miss him." Orion sighed. "I should be mad. But I know how hard you worked to give me the life I needed. To be there for me and run this place."

Jayne blinked back hot tears. "And now?"

She half expected him to hate her. To pile on guilt the way Charlie would when he had his energy back. The way Alexis seemed to want to do with her father.

She had friends whose children had broken their hearts, stolen from them, or walked out to "live their own lives." She'd built something with Orion, because at the end of the day, it had only been the two of them.

After he graduated high school, she'd focused on camp, knowing he needed time to live his life. The things he chose to do. The places he chose to go. All of it made her proud.

Everyone made mistakes, but God had done something in both of them.

She wiped away a tear. "This is insane. I can't believe he's here."

"He's a good guy. Knows his stuff," Orion said. "He probably saved Houston's life today." There was something else in his expression. She was about to ask what when he said, "He told me he had to turn his life around. He had no one. His ex-wife poisoned Alexis—"

Jayne cut him off. "Don't tell me his private business. Don't break a confidence."

"He's been sober for years." Orion stood. "You

39

should at least know that." Her son pulled her to him and kissed the top of her head. "You'll figure this out."

"What I *should* be doing is taking care of the camp kids in case we have to evacuate."

"I'll stick around as long as I can until I get ordered back to my team."

She nodded. "You're the best, Ry."

He grinned. "I know." His grin slipped and he winced. "I guess I should go talk to my father. See what he's doing." He looked down for a second. "What's Alexis like?"

Jayne gave herself a second, since her son had gained a father and a half-sister in one day. She was as much a mother as she was a girl who hadn't always made the right choices—and a camp counselor with a personal connection to one of her teens. "She's great." Jayne smiled. "She'll give us all a run for our money."

A firecracker tornado of teenage emotions wrapped up in grief. Determined to do amazing things in the world despite the fact Alexis felt like she'd never been handed anything for free in her life.

The situation between her parents seemed to have been complex. Some kids who came here had suffered, and she saw it on their faces. A few times she had called Child Protective Services when it'd become clear they were in danger at home and maybe they shouldn't go back there at the end of the summer.

Alexis might have some emotional or mental things to work through, but she had the grit to persevere.

Orion looked like he wanted to say something else.

When he didn't, she said, "I really am sorry you never had him in your life."

Her son, the man standing in front of her—the baby she had cared for and raised on her own—gave her another hug.

He stepped back.

The entire building rocked. Her painting of the mountains west of here rattled and then fell to the ground. Glass shattered.

Someone down the hall screamed.

FOUR

FLAMES LICKED INTO THE SKY, VISIBLE ABOVE THE trees before Charlie even turned the corner on the ATV. Just over a mile away thanks to the switchback in the road, he spotted it.

A propane truck on its side, fully engulfed. As he sped toward the vehicle, he assessed the whole scene and the area around it.

He pulled up, stopping the ATV at a safe distance, and dug out his phone, fumbling the buttons but managing to get the call going.

"Commander Dafoe."

Miles. "Commander, it's Charlie Benning. I need fire response to my location. There's a propane truck blocking the road up to the camp, fully engulfed. Possible casualties."

He didn't see the driver or another vehicle. How had it exploded?

The flames would die down when the natural gas had burned away, but by then it could be too late.

"Sparks and embers are hitting trees on both sides of the road." And all the campers were trapped up the hill. "If we don't get this thing suppressed, we'll have another wildfire on our hands."

"Copy that, Benning." Miles sounded like he was on the move. "We're stretched thin, and you're too far out from town resources. I'll call the BLM, but you and Price take the lead. This is what those kids train to do. They'll help."

A siren sounded behind him from the direction of camp.

Charlie twisted around to see an old rural fire truck pull up. The driver's door opened, and Orion jumped out. "Let's get to work, everyone."

Jayne jumped out of the passenger side and started calling out names. "Aria, Tiger, you're on the hose."

Miles said, "Anything else?"

Charlie turned back to the fire. "See if you can get me a retardant drop. It's not worth the risk of this getting away from us."

"I'll make the call."

"Thanks, Commander."

Miles hung up.

Orion came to stand by Charlie and nodded. "Good call."

"I don't like this." And he felt odd in wildland firefighting gear rather than the turnout coat and pants, helmet, and air tank he had carried for years.

Two of the teens raced by with a hose. Someone called back, and they knelt. Water jetted from the end of the hose. They worked with efficiency and competence.

Huh.

Alexis came over to him. "Here." She held out a

Pulaski. "We should do what we can to keep the trees from catching, right?"

"I'll get the chain saw." Orion jogged back to the truck.

"We need to clear anything that might bridge between the flames on the truck and the fuel in the forest."

Alexis ran for the front end of the truck, parked nose to the trees.

Charlie turned to Jayne, who had pulled a handkerchief over her mouth. "Guess that makes you incident commander." He jogged after Alexis toward the trees.

The engine hadn't blown, but the truck lay on its side perpendicular to the road. "We need to get the driver out."

"Then we'll need to get around the other side and make sure there are no other people here with injuries, right?" she said. "Once the fire is out, we can climb up and look in the cab."

"It'll be me doing that. Not someone whose guardian had to sign a waiver."

Alexis shot him a look.

The breather from that whole Jayne/Orion thing might taste a whole lot like fresh smoke, but being with her was what he'd wanted more than anything.

Alexis with him. It was all he'd ever wanted.

She held on to a Pulaski. "So, what do we do, boss?"

He chuckled. "Clear the ground."

Whoever maintained this road had done a solid job of getting brush off the shoulder. But where the trees began, the earth was swallowed up by thick bramble, with thorns that would shred clothes but which also grew ripe berries he had snacked on many times so far this summer.

"Clear the lower branches too. Right?"

He nodded. "That's right." Then he looked up where the front end of the truck almost touched a tree. "And we need to watch this oil leaking from the engine. Make sure that if it catches fire, we don't go up with it." He blew out a breath. "This should be a hazmat team, two fire trucks, and the fire chief on scene."

"Welcome to Montana." One of the teen boys strode over, his helmet drooping over one eye. "We do things ourselves up here."

Charlie said, "Dig a trench. Don't let that oil get to the pine needles. Got it?"

"Yes, sir." The kid dug his shovel into the ground.

Charlie looked at Alexis. "You good?"

"Uh, what?" Her cheeks flushed. The first sign of life he'd seen from her in months. Because of a boy?

Sure, there had been plenty of life in her when she'd told Orion he was her brother, but that had dissipated quickly.

Charlie had been on the cusp of figuring it out himself. But he hadn't put together who Orion was to him, so it hardly counted. He glanced back at Orion. His teammate and colleague.

His son.

On the far side of the street, Orion lopped branches off the tree. The top was already alight. They needed it to fall away from the other trees.

Charlie pulled off his gloves. He stuck two fingers in his mouth and whistled.

Orion turned. Charlie motioned to the tree, then

45

made a cutting motion and pointed at the middle of the street on the far side of the truck.

Orion nodded.

Jayne had the kids focused on the blaze. She patted the shoulder of the one battling flames with the hose. "Focus that to the front now. The dirt around the engine needs to be soaked."

Charlie left Alexis to her job, pulled his gloves back on, and climbed on the truck wheel, which radiated heat. He hauled himself up to the very top and looked over at the underside of the truck.

No second vehicle, like so many of the traffic fires he'd dealt with in his career. Accidents where one person had collided into another for varying reasons and caused a disaster. He turned and looked up the road, where Jayne stood watching him. Then at the ground around the truck.

This made no sense.

What on earth had caused the propane tank to explode before it could make its delivery and refill the camp tank? These things were designed to be as safe as possible.

He picked his way to the passenger door, which faced the sky. If the driver was still alive, Charlie could call for a helicopter.

Charlie pulled the handle and got the door open. He looked in. Winced.

The driver lay crumpled against the door at the bottom of the cab.

Charlie turned and caught Jayne's gaze. He shook his head.

"Heads up!" Orion repeated that two more times. "Tree falling!"

The burning tree shook, then started to ease over toward the ground, picking up speed as it fell.

It hit the dirt and gravel mix at the center of the road and exploded.

The ground sprayed up in a shower of dirt. Concussive force smacked Charlie, and he flew backward. *This is it.* At least he had the letter in his pocket for—

His body hit the dirt and he blinked up at the sky.

"Daaaaad!" Alexis slammed to her knees beside him.

He coughed. Black spots erupted like fireworks.

"You should breathe. You need to breathe, okay?"

The fire. The camp kids.

Jayne. Orion.

Charlie looked up at Alexis, who had tears in her eyes. Like the ones that he'd seen in Jayne's. Alexis gripped his hand. "Dad!"

He gasped, then coughed again. Then sucked in a breath. He focused on even breaths, in and out. Until he could say, "I'm good."

He gripped her hand and sat up, letting out a moan.

"Don't stand up. Just stay there." She held on to his hand.

"Charlie, you good?" Orion came over and crouched.

He managed to nod.

Someone said, "Land mine."

"What are you talking about, Tiger?" Alexis asked.

"That's what blew the tanker." One of the teens moved into view. "When I saw the tree blow, I

47

recognized it from a video I saw online. Someone buried a mine in the road, and it blew the tanker."

"More than one," Orion said. "If a second device blew the tree."

"Land mines?" Alexis shifted in her crouch. "What on earth?"

He'd been thinking the same thing. Charlie grunted. "Is the fire out?"

Jayne touched his shoulder. "Almost. What about the driver?"

"He didn't make it." Charlie looked around to where the teens worked the scene, clearing vegetation in danger of catching fire. Showing the level of training they'd had in their movements.

"We should request a medical chopper here. Get you taken to the hospital." Jayne sounded scared. "But if there are land mines in the road, we can't ask them to land and take the risk. We need to clear the area, backtrack our steps and get out of here."

Orion said, "The propane truck is blocking the road out. So unless we have a medical *emergency* on our hands, we might need to sit tight and wait."

"We don't."

Orion studied Charlie for a second, and Charlie wondered if he saw the intention in him. Orion said, "We can get you back to camp, at least. Have the nurse check you out?"

"His heart rate isn't too elevated."

He whipped his head around to Alexis. "That's why you're holding my hand?"

"I'm gonna check for a concussion now. Are you going to freak out about that too?" Alexis turned on the flashlight on her phone. "How does your head feel?"

He stared at her.

"What hurts, and how bad is it?" She shone the light in his eyes. "I know what I'm doing."

He blinked against the glare. "What is happening?"

"I'm trying to figure out if you gave yourself a concussion with that backward dive off the tanker that scared the life out of me."

Charlie touched her cheek with his glove. "Everything is going to be fine."

She scrunched up her nose. "You're supposed to tell me *you're* fine."

But he wasn't.

And they would both know it was a lie.

"Call your parents." A couple of kids groaned, but most already had contacted their folks. Jayne had sent out a text update to the listed parents in her files, informing them what happened with the tanker.

Orion had stayed with the ATV at the site so he could meet the emergency responders to pull the driver's body out. The rest of them had brought Charlie back so he could recuperate from taking that hit.

She'd checked on him a short time ago and found Alexis in there, the two of them having a quiet conversation that seemed serious.

Jayne had left them alone.

She faced the kids now, gathered in the common room where they had more than one kind of game console and a huge flatscreen TV. "Let your parents see your faces so they know you're okay. Walk around and show them all the safeguards we have in place that protect us from fire."

The oven buzzed from the kitchen behind her, loud enough that everyone heard it. She grinned. "And then we'll have chocolate cake."

A cheer went up.

"Dinner is in an hour."

Jayne headed back to the kitchen, where she had the trays already laid out. Ham. Cheese. Rolls. Butter. Always better after they'd been cooked in the oven.

Orion had told her that one of the hotshots made a mac and cheese that everyone apparently raved over.

She wondered if they'd hear about her sandwiches, but that was ridiculous. She didn't live in their world. She lived up here, where she didn't have to worry about who survived—or didn't.

At least, not before today, when Charlie flew through the air. Or before that, when she realized he was here, working as one of the Ember hotshots.

Sure, it should've hit her that Orion was in danger every day of summer. But she'd trained him more than the Ember fire command had. Her son knew how to keep himself safe.

So long as he didn't follow through with this crazy smokejumper idea.

The last thing she wanted was to bury him like she'd buried her father.

Stupid man.

That was what her mother had said about him. While the rest of Ember had hailed him a hero until she'd felt like she could walk a little taller and hold her head a little higher because she was his daughter.

He didn't care nothin' about us. He was just selfish. More interested in fire than his family.

The cake pan slammed on the wire rack a little too hard. Jayne hissed and squared it so the corner of the glass pan wasn't in the air. It needed to cool so she could frost it.

In the meantime, she would put the sandwiches together and check if they had enough chips for all the kids, since she'd been planning to head to the grocery store the day after tomorrow and stock up.

"Hey, need some help?" Bridget strode in and held her water bottle under the faucet at the big metal sink. She dumped the water and rinsed it inside and out.

"Did you get a chance to check on Charlie?"

"Some bruising on his back. Alexis filled me in on how he fell. I'm not surprised he got winded. I'm glad he's not as injured as he could've been—or should've been." Bridget leaned her hip against the front of the sink. "Can you believe, a land mine? What on earth?"

Jayne nodded, happy Bridget had waited until they were out of earshot of the kids before she shared that sentiment. "Orion said they have bomb-squad-trained firefighters in most places, but the best they could do here is a few of the hotshots along with the coroner. Apparently, these 'Trouble Boys' were military, so they know how to spot buried ordnances. He said the only thing better would be a bomb-sniffing dog."

Jayne smiled. "Also *apparently*...one of them knows this team, A Breed Apart. All working dogs, fully trained." She shook her head. "And I thought Aria's stories about Chevalier and her parents were crazy. Anyway, I guess the Trouble Boys are here, they wanna do it, and they're faster than flying in an expert."

Bridget said, "Now that would be something I'd like to see."

Jayne's head swam from everything. She'd been entirely too close to that explosion, and so had the kids. She did *not* want to see any more of it.

Instead, she pressed a hand to the front of her shirt and the necklace that hung under it. The one Orion had given her a few years ago on her birthday.

"Pretty hairy afternoon." Bridget shifted closer and unwrapped the ham, dumping it on the cutting board so she could start slicing it to the size of the rolls. "But everything turned out all right. Except for that driver."

Never mind the question of who on earth would do that. Or why. Had it been a targeted attack against the victim, or the camp?

Her mind kept replaying that image of Charlie flying back.

She'd been thanking God since then that no one else had been hurt. They had all been protected by the tanker from the force of the blast.

Her breath came fast.

Tears gathered in her eyes. She sniffed and held her breath before pushing it out slowly. *Get a grip, girl.*

"No one will blame you if you cry a little," Bridget said. "He could've died. I bet Orion is having a rough time as well right now."

Jayne gasped, trying to get ahold of herself. She'd nearly lost so much.

"He's the father of your son. You're allowed to freak out a little when he nearly died."

She shook her head. "I have to hold it together."

"Why?"

Jayne stared at her.

"Why can't you just let yourself fall apart for a second?"

She turned for the pantry. "I need to make the frosting."

Jayne swiped a tear from her face. She'd cried plenty of times, alone with a crying baby in the middle of the night. That was practically expected when your hormones were on a rollercoaster ride. Now she was supposed to be mature. In charge. The one who carried the weight of all the responsibility.

As much as she'd wanted someone to share it with over the years, that wasn't what God had given her.

Life was what it was. She thanked God for each day she had and the overflow of blessings He had given her. If she wanted something more than that, it flew in the face of the contentment she tried to live by.

"I'm just glad we're all okay here." She carried the powdered sugar back to the area with the mixer, strategically ignoring the disappointed look on Bridget's face. "So it's time to celebrate that. When Orion shows up, we can get this party started."

She headed for the big industrial refrigerator and the blocks of cream cheese.

"I'll be praying for the crew removing the body." Bridget shivered. "And no doubt Sheriff Hutchinson will be up here investigating soon enough."

Jayne glanced over. Bridget had been sweet on the sheriff for a long while.

"They'll get to the bottom of it."

Jayne was pretty sure she was supposed to be the one reassuring her friend. As camp director, she was responsible for morale as much as physical safety and learning.

Instead, Bridget was trying to reassure her.

"All I know is that we're up here until the road is clear. So it's time to pray the wind dies and the fire banks, or we'll be hunkered down while it rolls over us." She began to hum her favorite hymn.

If Jordan above me shall roll…

She'd read that verse this morning, the one where Paul said, "For to me to live is Christ, and to die is gain."

A hard thing when there was so much to do here. It might be gain for Charlie to go to heaven, but they would be left with grief and the promise of seeing each other again. The loss of so much of what could have been.

Thou wilt whisper thy peace to my soul. No matter what, she had God's peace by His Spirit.

She needed to talk with Alexis and ensure the girl would be all right. With no mother, if something happened to her father, she would surely be devastated. She would need people to come around her and support her through even more loss.

Jayne's chest tightened. She watched the frosting stir around in the mixer.

Losing Charlie? She didn't want to go through that all over again.

Orion was old enough he could make his own decision about the relationship he wanted with his father.

Jayne wasn't prepared to risk loss just for the chance that it might be nice to have him in her life again. Charlie didn't live here. He had two kids to focus on now. She would only get in the way and wind up being a drain on his time that he resented.

No. She wouldn't be demanding anything of him.

Not now, and not ever.

FIVE

EVEN THOUGH HE'D RATHER HAVE SACKED OUT ON A couch, Charlie had been relegated to a guest staff room that only had a bed, a desk and wooden chair, and a dresser. There had been something hanging on the wall earlier, but now it was just a hook. Some pieces of picture frame were in the trash can by the desk, but anything else had been swept away.

Alexis sat in the chair, which she'd pulled over to the side of the bed. Charlie had kicked off his boots and sat on the bed with his back to the wall. He could feel his eyelids wanting to close, but didn't let them.

"Jayne seems nice."

Alexis said, "Of course she is. She's great."

Because he had such good taste in women? Not hardly. She might be the one exception to that trend in his life. But that wasn't what he'd meant. Jayne had raised one child well already—which he took as a great sign that he'd been right on with his plan.

He was the one who had screwed up fatherhood.

Alexis would be well taken care of.

"She talks a lot about God and the Bible. I don't know much about that stuff." She adjusted her seat on

55

the chair. "But it sounds nice, and it means a lot to her to talk about it. You know how people have that... calm about them? They just don't get ruffled by everything happening in the world."

Charlie nodded. "I know people like that." Christians he worked with and was friends with. "They're good folks."

She stood. "You need anything?"

Charlie studied her. "I should be asking you that. Considering all the years I didn't work harder to make sure you had what you needed." He rubbed a hand on the Backdraft Pizza Grill T-shirt over his chest. "So no, I don't need anything, Lexi."

She looked away, her hands gripping the back of the chair. "Okay."

"Thanks for asking."

He spotted a tiny smile, and she tucked the chair back under the desk. "Goodnight, Dad."

Charlie's eyes closed before he heard her shut the door, but when his phone started to buzz in his pocket, he managed to put it on speaker. "Benning."

"It's Houston. Heard you got blown up."

Charlie chuckled. "Only a little. You fell through a hole in the ground."

"Doesn't sound nearly as interesting as a land mine."

It had probably hurt a whole lot less, though. At least he had his medicine tin in his pocket, or he would've been forced to have someone bring him more pills. That would reveal every secret he had and ruin his entire summer plan.

Now that he knew Jayne would do right by Alexis, he was even surer that he was on to something that would work.

Houston sighed. "Anyway, since I'm not back out until tomorrow, I was designated to sit in the office at Ember Fire HQ and call around with updates. So here goes. Orion held the scene until the Trouble Boys showed up, and then the sheriff and the coroner. They cleared the road around the truck, since the mines that exploded were close together."

"Any more mines?" Charlie hadn't heard any explosions.

"Nope. They got the body out of the truck and off to the morgue and didn't find any more explosives. But they also walked every inch of road around the truck and back, so we're sure the two were all that had been buried."

Charlie blew out a breath. "Not a job I'd have volunteered for." He'd probably have waited for the feds or the military to send a working dog that could sniff out explosives.

"Miles is finding a wrecker that can come to clear the propane truck from the road. We also have to ensure there are no unexploded land mines that were buried under where the truck is lying. So that might take time, even after we get something to haul it away."

"Given the size, it might need a flatbed semi to haul it away."

"I'll make a note of that for the report," Houston said. "Apparently there's a smokejumper with a connection to the ATF? But they're also talking to the National Guard. Whoever can get there faster to take care of it. Make sure no one else gets hurt."

"Good." The smokejumper was Logan, whose sister Andi had fallen hard for Jude—the ATF special agent. "As long as it's cleared."

"Orion reported the fire is out. He'll be back up at the camp soon. No need to stay out all night."

Charlie wanted to see his son. But what was he going to say? A hundred things rolled through his mind, each one sounding as dumb as the last.

"How are Alexis and the rest of the kids?"

"They were great today." He'd been blown away by the caliber of their training. "And Alexis is good. Came by to talk to me without any prompting. Just wanted to sit and visit."

"That's great."

"Hey, later in the summer…will you chat with her? She might have questions about Jesus and faith. All that stuff. Can you answer them for her?" For him too. "Can you make sure she's on the right path?"

"Sure I will," Houston said. "But why can't you do that?"

Charlie tried to think of an answer. He wasn't as clued in as Pastor Houston James, but Houston wasn't going to accept that as a good reason.

"Does this have to do with that thing with the nurse?"

"I've got it covered." Those words had become a refrain. Despite what had cropped up the last couple of days: seeing Jayne, finding out about Orion. How things were turning out still wasn't bad. At least, not as bad as they could've been.

"Is that true?"

Charlie said, "Don't worry about me. Just make sure Lexi is going to be all right."

"All right." Houston spoke quietly. "Sounds like Jayne plans to carry on as normal. They wouldn't be headed to town as a group for a few weeks anyway. We can bring a chopper up there with any needed supplies, or if we've got to airlift someone out."

Jayne.

Charlie's energy level slipped to the floor. He let out a long sigh.

"What's going on, Charlie? You good?"

"Just tired." His eyes were drifting closed.

"Is that really all it is?"

He might as well give the pastor something to pray about. "Jayne and I...it was a long time ago. We were seventeen." He tried saying it out loud. "I only found out today. Orion is my son."

"Brother...wow. That's...I don't even know what to say."

Charlie chuckled, not even opening his eyes. "That about sums it up."

"I'll be praying for you. Let God guide it. Let Him give you the words to say. After you get some sleep."

"Thanks."

"Take care, yeah?"

The phone beeped.

Charlie drifted, not even bothering to slide down onto the bed. He slept propped up against the walls, having fitful dreams where Orion turned away from him, and seconds later, flames swallowed everything.

He woke up in semidark, a little light from the hall spilling under the door.

He took a couple of pills he should take before bed—if he slept a normal schedule—with the bottled water on the nightstand. If the pattern held, he wouldn't sleep again for a few hours.

Plenty of time to walk off the aches of the day.

He decided to check out the camp, since land mines could mean anything and there was no security up here. Did they have a way to protect themselves? He strode out of the hall and into the common area and looked around.

Gleaming kitchen, visible through the open cafeteria window.

Shiny counters.

Chairs overturned on the table. Clean floor underneath.

He scanned the living area and stopped short. A popular sci-fi TV show he'd never watched but knew plenty about now played on the screen. Jayne lay on the couch, holding a tissue to her nose.

She spotted him and gasped, scrambling up to sitting, and immediately pointed at him. Tears streamed down her face. "Not a word out of you. It's a good show!"

Charlie lifted his hands. "I happen to have it on good authority that *Trek of the Osprey* is the best show *ever*. And I'm prepared to cite my sources." He shrugged one shoulder and lowered his hands. "Ever heard of *Spenser Storm*?"

Jayne folded her arms. "Spenser Storm? You expect me to believe you know him?"

Charlie grinned. He dug out his phone and came over to show her the screen.

She stared at the picture of four hotshots—including Charlie *and* Orion—with Spenser in the center. "You know him."

"Hate to burst your bubble, but he's crazy in love with Emily." He waved his phone. "The blonde in the middle. She's nuts over him too, so it works."

"Spenser Storm is dating a wildland hotshot?" She absolutely loved that idea.

Charlie shrugged his shoulder. "They were shooting a movie nearby a few weeks ago, with that superstar Winchester Marshall there and everything. Emily was the hotshot assigned to oversee fires on set. They fell pretty hard for each other—out a second story window, actually."

Jayne chuckled. "I'd like to hear that story."

"It's happened a couple more times since. One of the guys, Houston? He fell for Sophie."

"Sophie Lamb? She runs the horse rescue place just outside Ember?"

Charlie nodded.

"I love her." She folded her arms. "Is he a good guy?"

"Youth pastor. His brother is my chief. *Was* my chief. In Last Chance County."

"Where you worked rescue squad?" Orion had filled her in on some other details when he got back. He'd peeked in on his dad, but Charlie had been sleeping. They'd both decided to leave him alone. Except Jayne hadn't been able to go to her room and pretend like everything was fine. Her mind had been spinning far too much to rest.

So she'd opted for her guilty pleasure—sci-fi reruns.

"Yep. Fifteen years on rescue squad."

"That's amazing."

"Usually this is when people ask why I never made lieutenant."

"I'd like to know everything about you. But not because I think you should have hit some arbitrary standard."

"It's really just my same job but with a bunch of paperwork."

Why was he staring at her like that—as if she was some kind of unknown thing? After all they'd shared? He knew her better than he thought he did.

She focused back on what they'd been saying. "Lieutenant would probably be a pay raise too."

"Money that Helena would've had taken out of my paycheck by the court so she could 'take care of Alexis.' By going to Hawaii with her friends for 'self-care' and leaving Alexis at home. All so she could be the best mom she could be because she was living her best life."

Jayne frowned.

"Sorry." He rubbed a hand through his sleep-rumpled hair. "I probably sound bitter. But you always did bring the honest truth out of me."

"I'd rather have that than a lie."

"Bad relationship?"

She shook her head. "It's just been me."

"Since…"

She nodded. Since him.

"I know we didn't leave it in a good place. I had to go home, and you were going to high school here. I wasn't mature enough to handle what we had. But I didn't want you to be alone all these years."

"I wasn't alone. I had Orion." She sat backward on the arm of the couch, her elbow on the head cushion. "I wanted to be the best mom I could be. Nothing like mine."

She didn't want to get into the past. At least, not that part of it. So she said, "I was working here and not going to town much except for supplies. I wasn't going to waste money on a babysitter just to go out and waste money on food and drink that would make me grumpy the next day." She shrugged. "Orion deserved better than that."

Charlie said, "Sounds like you did right by him. He's an amazing kid. And a crazy-good firefighter."

Who wanted to be a smokejumper. Someone who fell out of planes. *On purpose.* The idea filled her with so much dread she wanted to be sick. Enough that she had to turn away so Charlie didn't see the honest truth on her face.

She spotted her phone on the coffee table and picked it up. Frowned. "Nothing."

"What's wrong?"

She turned to him. "There's a guy staying in one of the hill cabins. I told him about our status update. That he should be ready to leave when they upgrade us to 'go,' but he never responded. I'm worried about him. He's a bit of a loner."

Charlie said, "Do you want to walk up the hill and make sure he's okay?"

She hadn't wanted to go by herself, and Orion had been exhausted. But Charlie had napped. "If you feel up to walking a few miles."

"I've got some in me." He patted his chest. "I'm not so old and broke down that I can't sneak out after dark with you like the good old days."

She giggled. "We still frown on that kind of behavior, you know." That was how Alexis had put it together that Orion was her half-brother.

"I promise I'll keep my hands to myself."

Thankfully the kids all slept within the main house—girls on the upper floor with the balcony, and boys on the basement level that led out to the hot tub on the back patio. They were all hunkered down for the night, though she knew some of the guys were still watching a movie in their common area. The Masterson twins' parents were in a different time zone, so they were waiting for their parents to wake up so they could call.

Charlie stopped on the porch so she could click the front door shut.

Overhead, a moth buzzed around the porch light. The smell of wildfire smoke hung in the air. She could hear the river from what she referred to as her "front yard" even though it was the driveway. Or the main drag through camp.

"You could've knocked me over with a feather, seeing that fire truck pull up behind me today and y'all jump out." He grinned.

She went first off the front steps, wearing her muck boots. What was the point in trying to dress up? It was so dark she had to light their way with a flashlight, and it wasn't like she was trying to impress Charlie by being something she wasn't. Why wear fashionable shoes?

He'd asked her about relationships, but so what? Now he knew she had no one. About the saddest story ever told. But she liked her life.

She'd raised her son.

Trained group after group of kids.

Seen some of them become firefighters, now friends who emailed her every once in a while so they could catch up.

Charlie clicked his flashlight on. "Smells the same. Sounds the same."

"Looks a little older, though."

He nudged her. "Speak for yourself."

She laughed and shoved at his shoulder. "Oh, I

should've asked you if you needed something to eat. Were you hungry?"

He shrugged. "I'm good."

"Alexis did say you've lost weight. I get busy and focused and forget to eat." She maybe should've done that more, and then she wouldn't look so much like a middle-aged mom. Jayne sighed. "It's this way."

She strode ahead of him, hanging a right at the old tree and hitting the trail that snaked up the hillside. Anyone that stayed here had to pack in and pack out. No electricity. Running water that was as cold as the stream. The food you ate was the food you carried in. Fire pit. Lanterns that were powered by battery.

It was a great place to be off the grid.

Except when the camp had to be evacuated because of a wildfire.

"There's just one of these?" Charlie said. "I remember several, is that right?"

"Only one is currently occupied." She scanned the dark with her flashlight. "And pretty hard to find if you don't know what you're looking for."

"Who's the guest?"

"Roger Kirkpatrick. He seemed familiar, like I've seen him before. He showed up with cash a couple of weeks ago, and I ran his ID. The sheriff didn't have his name pop with anything."

"Good call. Can't be too careful these days."

Jayne said, "A lot of the time, I just go with my gut. I let the Lord lead me in how I feel about my read on a person. He didn't raise any red flags with me."

She reached the end of the trail that opened to the cabin and the land around it. Maybe an acre total, tucked in the woods. A great hideaway—or romantic getaway spot.

Not that she'd ever have need of one. But she was with Charlie. Those thoughts came naturally, and she'd have to work to avoid slipping back there if they spent much more time together.

Neither of them was the person they'd been years ago. Right now she just wanted to get to know her son's father—which was probably what Orion also wanted to do.

"The front entrance is over here." She rounded the cabin and saw the door open.

Stopped.

"I'll go first." Charlie touched her shoulder, then stepped past her to jog up the four steps and push the door open. "Somebody was here. Looks like they left in a hurry." He stuck his head out, a dark look on his face. "But they didn't take their stuff."

Jayne turned to scan the dark woods around them.

The flashlight snagged on an animal, low to the ground in trees, red eyes in the artificial glow. "I don't like this. He could be in trouble."

SIX

CHARLIE PEEKED AT THE BREAKFAST CASSEROLES HE had assembled and then closed the oven. *He could be in trouble.* Plenty of that had been going on the past few weeks, but being here at Wildlands Academy felt like a reprieve from it.

Now there could be a man in danger close by.

As he straightened, pain lanced through his lower back. No one was around, so he gave himself a moment to be honest. Braced both hands against the edge of the counter and bowed his head. He groaned against the pain.

The fatigue.

The unfairness of it all. Not just being diagnosed with a treatable disease—but the fact that it was one that meant giving up everything he was and asking Alexis to jeopardize her own future just to save his life.

He wasn't worth it.

And the fact that he'd never be a firefighter again? He should walk over the ridge and into the flames right now.

One tiny problem? He was scared to death of

doing it. Feeling all that pain. Knowing he'd chosen to end his life.

Even if he'd reasoned it was the only worthwhile avenue for everyone he knew, he still couldn't imagine the anguish he'd have to be under to finally bring himself to go through with it. But if he waited more than another few weeks, it might be too late. He'd have to jump in his truck and find a canyon or bridge to go over.

Give Alexis the chance to make the future she wanted.

Save Orion from having to learn how much of a screwup he was.

Jayne…

He had no idea what he even wanted to feel about her, but it felt like all those old feelings had stirred to life again after being dormant for so long. As if they'd never really gone away. He'd missed so much of the good years of her life and the time he'd been healthy. Called a hero.

He wanted to be that man for her, but it would never happen.

But the fact was, her life wouldn't be better with him in it. She'd been so scared the night before. The last thing he wanted was to cause her grief. He'd be piling more on Alexis, but he knew she was strong enough to handle it.

He refused to be a burden.

Charlie was going to go out on his terms. His choice.

No matter what anyone else thought. He would do what he had to do.

Nothing would change his mind and leave him hurting Alexis more than he had so many times already.

"Everything okay?"

He straightened, trying not to let on that even that hurt. Charlie said, "Breakfast is almost ready."

"That's not what I asked." Orion lifted a coffee mug to his lips.

"I didn't sleep all that great." True enough.

"You're not hiding as much as you want to believe you are." Orion leaned against the wall by the door, where Charlie had found the meal plan that said omelets for today. "I didn't put it together until Alexis said what she did about you having lost weight. I had figured it was the physical exertion of being a hotshot, but it's more than that, isn't it?"

Charlie stared at his son. "Yes."

No pretense. No lies.

"Is there anything I can do?"

Charlie reached into the pocket of his pants and pulled out a metal tin. He shook it, which made the medication inside rattle. "I'm good for a few days. But if this goes on any longer than that, I'll need to get back to the Ember base camp and get more meds."

They'd worked together for long enough that a professional rapport had developed between them. Things were different now that he knew Orion was his son.

"I'm sorry I never got to see you grow up. I missed out on everything, and I'll go to my grave regretting not being able to be your father."

"It wasn't Mom's fault."

The kid wanted to defend Jayne, which meant he loved her enough to do what he could to protect his mom. "What did she tell you about me?"

Orion looked at the mug in his hands. "That you

were both far too young. That you both had issues you needed to deal with. She said it was better if you got to live your life."

Better for him. Not better for her that she didn't have to contend with a baby and Charlie's problems?

"Don't be mad at her."

Charlie sighed. "What would be the point in that? What's done is done." And they were stuck here for the time being. His life was too short to hold a grudge to the end.

"So you don't resent that she basically kept you from knowing me?"

"I'm not going to make her life miserable over her choice." He didn't have enough time left, or the energy, to do that.

Orion stared at him. "All right." He nodded. "I checked in with Miles. They're deploying us with the team close enough that we can hike from here and meet up with them. But they're going to go assess first. See what the conditions are like."

"You don't want to stick around here at camp? Make sure your mom and everyone stays out of danger?"

Orion said, "If we meet up with the team, we get to keep the fire from coming anywhere near this place."

So his mom hadn't told him about the missing camper? She had told Charlie she would call the sheriff first thing in the morning and report him missing. Charlie wanted to go walk around the cabin in the daylight, right after breakfast. Make sure the man hadn't been hurt and wasn't lying somewhere they hadn't been able to see in the dark.

If Orion wanted to protect the home he'd grown

up in by doing his job, that wasn't a bad thing. "Good deal. But I plan on being here until I'm ordered otherwise."

"This isn't a vacation."

Charlie glanced aside at Orion, wondering what the kid was thinking. "You okay? You saw a dead body yesterday. It was pretty gruesome inside that truck cab. Can't have been much better seeing it up close."

Orion shrugged. "Mack and I cleared debris. The other Trouble Boys took care of the body."

So Ham, Mack's older brother, had made sure the two young guys on the hotshot team hadn't come face-to-face with something they didn't need to see.

And they'd let him protect them like that. Knowing full well why Ham had put them on clean-up duty.

"This camp has a fire truck. Does it have anything that would help us move that propane truck from where it's blocking the road?"

Orion shook his head. "Couple ride-on lawn mowers. Those two ATVs, and a snowplow attachment. The fire truck has a winch, but it's not going to shift a vehicle that size."

"I guess we're waiting for Miles to get it towed, then."

Orion said, "The wind is going to shift today. Another front is coming down from Canada. We might have to take the kids up to meet our team if it's bad enough they need help."

Charlie hadn't checked the morning fire forecast and weather report. "You think things could get dicey?"

"Miles requested all the planes he could, but

there's a blaze in Idaho they're covering this morning before the heat of the day. We're a lower priority unless something changes."

"And the helicopter from yesterday?"

Orion said, "Both of them are focusing on the south and west. Since the fire burned through that campground, everyone wants it kept away from residences. It's up to our team to cut a line to protect the camp."

"And we're going to be pushing hard against the wind all day."

He nodded. "Miles said the helicopters might even have to be grounded later today if conditions get too bad."

Charlie pulled one casserole out, then the other. The smell of onion, bacon, and cheese hit his nose, and his stomach grumbled for once. A positive sign that he might actually feel like eating a whole meal.

He needed the energy.

Orion came over. "Those smell amazing."

"The Crawford breakfast special."

"Like Logan, the smokejumper?" There was a whole lot of hero worship in Orion's eyes.

"His brother. My lieutenant, Bryce Crawford." Charlie said, "I can teach you how to make it."

"Sweet." Orion said, "Are you going to stick around here at the end of summer? Or are you going back to Last Chance County?"

Not quite the hero worship, as when he'd been talking about Logan, but not nothing. Charlie didn't know what to say, though. He couldn't make any plans for the future.

Not now, and not ever.

He couldn't say, *I don't know where I'll be.* Or, *We'll see how it goes.* Because neither of those would be true.

"Or do you have something else lined up? You're not staying here, and you're not going home either?" Orion frowned. "What are you going to do?"

Charlie hesitated.

"I'll ask Alexis. At least she'll tell me the truth."

"I've never lied to you."

"Then don't start now." Orion set his cup down hard. "Are you staying or not?"

He didn't know what to say. After weeks of being colleagues, this new dynamic was odd, to say the least. How was he supposed to explain that he'd come here for the summer not expecting to do anything at all at the end of the season?

"If you can't even give me an honest answer that you don't know"—Orion stepped back and headed for the door—"then forget it."

Charlie watched him go, the ache in his chest intensifying as his son moved out of view.

The bell for meals rang.

It was better this way. Better not to get too close when it would be over soon anyway.

Orion couldn't miss what he'd never had.

Jayne eyed Charlie and took another bite. "Who did you say came up with this?"

He had that knowing look on his face that got her into so much trouble as a seventeen-year-old. "Lots of meals in the firehouse are called 'what's in the fridge.' That's all this is, really."

She nodded, then swallowed the bite, trying to

figure out what seasonings he'd added to get a simple breakfast casserole to taste like this.

"What did the sheriff say about your guest up the hill?"

"He was out on a call, so I left a message and chatted with the receptionist for a bit." Jayne knew her from a ladies' Bible study she'd attended in the spring.

Orion sat at the long cafeteria table, and all the kids had settled in groups to eat breakfast, chatting, laughing. Someone had put the weather channel on the TV, but it wasn't showing anything near enough to Ember to help them with the day's fire forecast.

"Do you still want to go look around that cabin?" Charlie asked. "See if we just missed that guy 'cause it was dark?"

She nodded. "I want to be sure he's actually missing if we're going to make the sheriff drive all the way up here." Which meant she couldn't teach the kids this morning. "Orion, could you take the training class until morning break?"

Orion glanced at Charlie, an expression on his face she recalled from second grade when one of the other kids had stolen his basketball. A kind of angry, upset thing she didn't know how to fix. He scraped his chair back and walked to the calendar on the wall.

Sparky got up and shook himself off, padding over on those four spindly legs behind her son.

Today was buddy rescue drills and then a lecture on cloud formations. He ruffled Sparky's head and came back to pick up his plate. "I'll cover it."

Jayne twisted in her seat to look at Charlie, recalling now that she'd sat first. Then Orion. Charlie had come along later and purposely sat beside Orion, who hadn't even looked at him. "What was that about?"

Charlie got up, looking a whole lot like Orion had when he did the same thing just a moment ago. "Let's go look for that guy." He took his half-empty plate, dumped the uneaten food, and set the dish in the bin to be washed. He turned to stare at her, probably because she hadn't followed him.

Jayne ate the last couple of bites. Alexis took her dishes with a grin, handing Jayne a soapy, wet rag in exchange. She washed this long table, then the others. Four kids were already halfway done washing the dishes. She checked in with them, but by now they knew the drill. "Thanks, guys."

She walked out to where Charlie waited by the kitchen door. "Do you always pitch in?"

"Do you always quit your meal unfinished and leave to go do something?"

He hesitated. "Hazard of being a firefighter at a busy house, I guess. I can't count the number of meals I haven't finished over the last twenty years."

They headed outside, following the same path they'd taken the night before. Four deer—a doe and three fawns—grazed in the field by the river. If they followed the river they'd reach the lake, but this path sent them up the side of the hill.

She glanced at Charlie, wondering about that pinched look on his face. "So, why give up rescue squad to come here for the summer?"

She knew Alexis's mom had passed away over the winter. Maybe the girl just needed a break from her life for the summer. But it also looked a whole lot like Charlie might've wanted to dump her somewhere she'd be watched out for, occupied with a training program while he still got to fight fires.

"We needed a change of scenery."

Jayne lifted a branch and stepped under it. If fire rolled through this section of forest, it could be devastating. The whole place was dry from months of drought. They couldn't clear the forest floor of every bit of brush.

All they could do was protect lives. Property was always the secondary concern.

"And Alexis wants to be a firefighter?"

"Actually, I think last she said a paramedic, but only because that's faster than being an RN."

Jayne chuckled. "I recall her saying something to that effect." Still, Jayne wasn't sure it had been Alexis's idea for her to come here. "We do cover some medical aspects of firefighting and basic rescue scenarios. Like what they're doing today." She glanced back, but it didn't look as though Charlie was going to say anything.

He looked deep in thought. Or in pain.

She didn't know him well enough anymore to figure out which it was.

"I'm glad Orion agreed to take the class this morning. The kids respond better to him than they do an old lady like me because he's closer to their age."

"If you're old, then so am I."

She stopped to scan the area around the cabin. Charlie did the same—standing much closer to her back than she'd have thought was necessary. She glanced over her shoulder and found his face. Close.

Having him here was such a surprise after not seeing him for so many years. Not only because it meant Orion could meet his father but because she got to know Charlie now, as an adult. Sober. Wiser. Steady like an old oak—though she didn't think he would appreciate that description.

He looked down at her mouth. "What's funny?"

Something moved at the edge of her awareness. "I'll tell you later."

She stepped away from him and tried to find whoever she'd seen just now—or whatever it had been, though she didn't think it had been an animal.

"I saw someone over there." She pointed in the right direction.

"Let's keep walking."

His voice had an odd tone. She wasn't sure what to make of it. "Is there something going on?"

"I figured the sheriff might've filled you in at some point, but there was a murder a few weeks back, and before that, the explosion in a trailer, or cabin, which initially started the fire."

She scanned the ground as she walked so they didn't pass Roger and miss him. "I think I heard about the murder. But why would that have anything to do with my guest?"

"Who knows? The whole thing has me on edge." Charlie sighed. "There's this smokejumper, Booth. He tells the craziest stories, and they've gotten in my head. Houston and Sophie found that body they thought was her brother, and Dakota and Allie found those kids who saw that guy get popped."

She turned back, one eyebrow up.

"That's how they say it!" He looked completely exasperated. "Dakota used to be a cop. I don't wanna hear another SWAT story the rest of my life."

Jayne pressed her lips together to keep from laughing. Charlie was going to be an adorable grandpa, all grumpy old man. She thought it was cute.

"Anyway, the guy's name is Earl. Some local thug around Ember, and he's got a brother, I guess. Floyd. They double-crossed a cartel, so there was no way for them to get cheap drug shipments from south of the border. They had to start making it themselves again. One of the hotshots—Emily, who is dating your TV boyfriend now—"

"Spenser Storm is not my TV boyfriend! He's practically Orion's age."

Charlie chuckled as they approached the cabin. "The guy who Earl murdered turned out to be an ex-Army Ranger or some kind of clandestine operative the government is denying all knowledge of?" He said it like a question. "Dakota has been following the case after Houston and Sophie found the body in the woods. Everyone is interested since I guess it involves Sophie's brother."

"I'm used to being out of the loop because I'm up here most of the time. I only go down to town for supplies, but all this actually makes me want to stay up here more and *not* get involved."

"Good call," Charlie said. "Keep yourself and those kids safe."

They agreed about that, at least.

She searched the cabin again and came out to find Charlie sitting on the front step. "He's not inside, but if he left, he didn't take any of his stuff with him. I can't tell if he slept here last night or not."

She wanted to sit by Charlie, but they needed to keep looking. "I hope he's not hurt. Or out here somewhere all alone."

"I'm sensing a theme with you." Charlie stood,

touching her waist in a comforting gesture. "You take care of people. You worry about them being safe."

"I've prayed for you a lot over the years and made a lot of 'unspoken' prayer requests."

He shook his head. "What does that mean?"

"Just that I didn't want to share what was private."

"But you prayed, and you had other people praying?"

She nodded.

"You realize that probably saved my life, right?" He wound his arms around her waist.

She held on to him, her hands just above his elbows—not wanting to venture too far. They'd barely just met each other again.

"More than once would be my guess." He studied her. "You ever have that feeling someone is praying for you because you have no idea where the peace you have is coming from?"

She could use some of that peace right now. Her heart pounded so hard she could hear it in her ears.

Behind her, to the east, she heard the crack of a branch.

A gunshot exploded through the trees.

Charlie whipped her around, and they fell into the cabin. He covered her with his body as bullets zipped through the air above them.

SEVEN

PAIN RIPPED THROUGH CHARLIE'S RIGHT SIDE. He groaned and had to roll over—off Jayne—so he didn't collapse on her. The gunshots cut off abruptly.

He stared at the ceiling and tried to breathe through the pain. He'd seen the man's face and a ponytail of hair that'd told him exactly who it was.

Someone yelled. Another shot cracked outside, but it didn't hit the cabin like the others all had. *Someone is trying to kill you.* But who, and why? And had the target been him, Jayne, or both of them? This could be about getting rid of the camp director specifically for all he knew...or something entirely different.

He glanced over. *You okay?* The words wouldn't take hold, but he mouthed them.

She leaned over him. Touched his face. "Charlie?"

He could only gasp a breath.

"Did you get shot?"

Certainly felt like it. "No." He breathed. *Come on.* The last thing he needed was for her—or anyone else—to realize he wasn't as fine as he claimed. But

80

getting up would be just about impossible for the next few seconds.

She felt around his torso and under his sides. "I don't see blood."

"I didn't get shot." He'd just jarred everything in his back, and his failing kidneys showed no mercy. Charlie squeezed his abs and planted his elbows. Managed to get up that far.

She lifted an envelope with her name on it. "What is this?"

Charlie snatched it so fast he nearly landed on his back again. He ignored how much it hurt and stuffed the letter into his pocket. Now that he'd met Jayne again, he should rewrite it. Explain better so she wasn't as confused at the end of summer.

The fact was, he'd nearly been shot just now.

Charlie could have stepped into the path of one of those bullets and taken the hit. Ended it all. No more pain and suffering...for him.

And yet instinct had him diving on Jayne. Keeping her from being shot had saved both of their lives.

A wasted opportunity, depending on how he looked at it. But ideally, no one would witness his death—then he could keep the truth a secret.

"Talk." Jayne eyed him. "Why do you have an envelope with my name on it in your pocket?"

Charlie needed to get up, not be dragged into this.

"You were going to leave me a note?" Jayne backed up and stood.

They needed to make sure they were safe. Not get into a discussion.

Too bad he didn't have it in him to stand yet. He had to sit here, close enough he could shift over and lean his back against a bookshelf of battered paperback thrillers. The lamp above teetered a little, then settled. There was a bullet hole in the lampshade. More bullet holes in the wall on the far side. The gas camp stove was on the floor, and the coffee pot lay askew nearby.

"I think you should tell me what that was." She stood by the front door, effectively taking cover. Apparently not so worried about what had gone on outside—and had since moved away from them, given what he'd heard.

"It's just a letter." He blew out a breath. "It's not for now, and you don't need to worry about it."

"What's going on with you, Charlie?"

He'd never been able to turn down that look in her eyes. He pulled the tin from his pants pocket. "Can you get me a glass of water?"

She pushed off the wall and came back with a cup.

He swallowed two pills.

"What do you have?"

He tucked the tin back in his pocket. "It's my kidneys."

"And no one knows?" She folded her arms.

He shook his head. "I don't want Alexis to find out." Before she could object, he said, "You didn't see her with her mother. It was a messed up situation before Helena was diagnosed with cancer. It got worse. Alexis watched her mother deteriorate, and Helena made everyone's lives miserable every minute of it. Manipulating Alexis. Trying to do it with me. Twisting the doctors and nurses into it, weaving a web."

He wanted to believe his daughter was smart enough to see through the façade, but that would only make it so much worse for Alexis. She would realize just how much her mom had delighted in manipulating everyone around her—often for no reason other than that she could.

"I'm not going to let her watch me die as well."

"Good." Jayne nodded. "But is fighting wildland fires really what you should be doing? Seems like you might be better off on medical leave. Do you…need the money?"

"It's not about that." He couldn't even tell her out loud what he planned to do. She agreed with his choice to not cause Alexis more pain. Most likely, she thought he intended to fight to live.

The truth was quite different.

She would never agree it was the right thing. And apparently his instincts felt the same, driving him to dive out of the way of bullets.

Which made him wonder…would he be able to go through with it?

But the alternative would be to drag Alexis into watching another drawn-out medical battle. She couldn't handle that. Her mother's death had broken her in a way he would never be able to fix. His daughter needed to be free to live her life, not dragged into his problems. He would never let her give up a kidney for him. Not when she would suffer for years with the repercussions.

It could ruin her life.

A tiny niggle in the back of his mind wanted to point out that he had Jayne here with him. That he had Orion, a guy Charlie desperately wanted to get to know—but never would. That he'd never get the chance to see Alexis fall in love or walk her down the aisle to the man she chose to spend the rest of her life with.

Plenty of reasons to fight.

But he couldn't take the risk he would mess their lives up all over again. The way he had so many times before.

He'd been so certain. Instead, now it seemed like God wanted to offer him a choice.

Charlie managed to stand. "Let's get back to camp. We need to make sure whoever was outside didn't go that way."

Jayne frowned but came outside with him. "From the direction of the crashing through the brush, it sounded like they ran off toward the ravine, away from camp."

They had only walked a few steps before she said, "You good?"

"I will be after I call Dakota and get him to send me the photo he has of the guy the sheriff is trying to find." Had it really been the same guy?

"You saw the shooter."

He nodded.

"That's not good."

He touched her shoulder. "We'll be okay. Someone protected us, and we're going to be smart about safety now."

As long as no one else got hurt.

At least he knew they hadn't brought danger up here with them. Instead, it seemed like they'd come just in time to make sure the kids stayed safe. "Did the guy who rented the cabin have a ponytail?"

"No, he had short, dark hair. I have a copy of his driver's license in my records. I'll show you."

They emerged on the far side of camp to a bunch

of commotion and cheering. Charlie nearly reacted but caught himself when he realized it was the kids and a bunch of hotshots.

Two lanes and a cheering section. Orion had a hose and periodically sprayed the contestants in the face while they were dragging dummies across the gravel down the lanes, then raised it to rain down on them.

Jayne chuckled. "That's not exactly what the training schedule says."

Charlie only had eyes for Alexis. She hauled her dummy to the end of the line, just a fraction slower than the hotshot—the youngest of the bunch, Mack. The other Trouble Boys hollered from beside the kids.

Mack and Alexis high-fived, then lowered their hands. Still clasped. The touch lingered a little longer than it needed to before they separated, and two camp kids jumped up to take a turn.

Alexis spotted him and grinned.

That was a smile he'd never thought he'd see again.

And pretty soon he wouldn't get the chance. Ever. Unless he changed the whole plan.

One of the hotshots strode over to meet them. Given how Charlie seemed to struggle to walk, she pointed at the porch chairs. "Let's sit down." She sighed long as she settled into it.

The hotshot said, "You good?"

"It's been a day already."

Charlie settled in the chair beside her. The hotshot leaned against the rail. Built in a way that looked like he'd been carved out of stone, he had a square jaw and the bluest eyes she'd ever seen. If it wasn't for his eyes, he would look lethal with that tight haircut and the tattoos on his forearms. His sleeves were pushed up past his elbows, and she spotted TROUBLE inked onto the blade of his forearm.

Wasn't that the truth.

He reached over and shook her hand. "Hammer."

"Jayne Price."

"Camp director." A dark-featured man with his hair pulled back in a bun ascended the stairs but kept his distance. "And Orion's mom."

"That's me." She nodded.

The dark-featured man glanced at Charlie, then at her, a tiny smile on his face. Over in the gravel, the kids started to chant. "Ti-ger, Ti-ger, Ti-ger…"

Two more boys raced, pulling weighted dummies along the strip they'd marked out.

Alexis sat with the others, but the youngest hotshot Jayne had ever seen stared at the teen like he wanted the courage to go talk to her.

Charlie showed her a picture on his phone. "Is this the guy you rented to?"

Ponytail. Still, she shook her head. "No. That's not him." It could be their shooter, though. "Is it who you saw?"

He nodded. "That's the guy." He stowed his phone. "Dakota said everyone else is headed here as well."

Hammer said, "That's right. Commander Dafoe doesn't like the weather conditions. We scouted the fire this morning, and it could move this way if the wind picks up this afternoon."

Once night fell again, the fire would reduce to a

slumber with the cool temperatures. But it was the high afternoon temps that would be the most dangerous, especially with unpredictable winds.

Jayne scanned the camp. She would stand behind the preparations they'd made, but a fire could still tear through the area. The cabins she rented would be destroyed. Lives could be lost. People. Animals. The dangers were numerous.

Charlie said, "The fire is ten miles from here. How'd you get over here so fast?"

Quiet guy by the porch steps said, "We jogged."

Charlie chuckled. "Of course you did."

Hammer said, "Once we all meet up, we'll head back out there and start working up a defensive line."

He didn't speak like a hotshot. More like a guy with military background, which matched his bearing—and that of his friends. Except the youngest one, now staring longingly at Alexis when no one was watching. Meanwhile, Orion seemed to be soaking everyone at this point, whether they were competing in the training exercise or not.

"We floated the idea of a prescribed burn, but the conditions are too temperamental. Miles doesn't want to risk it getting out of control."

Jayne liked Miles Dafoe, the Ember Fire Commander, a whole lot. "If it does jump your line, could you steer it toward the lake? Let the fire burn out when it hits the water." Fire needed fuel. There was plenty of heat and oxygen out here in the Montana mountains. What they had to do was starve it of fuel.

Charlie said, "Good idea."

One of the kids jumped up, Samuel Masterson. "Uncle Dakota!" He ran for the group of hotshots that came into view up the lane. His twin, Joshua, raced after him.

Tiger Christiansen headed over as well, and he did that bro-hug thing guys did with Conner Young, the hotshot crew chief.

"Small world." Hammer seemed almost wistful about that.

Charlie chuckled. "I've noticed."

She watched the hotshots greet the kids, who basically hero-worshipped the lot of them. Two female hotshots drew the girls to them. They'd be peppered with questions and asked for stories—at least, until the smokejumpers showed up. Then they all were swept up in awe of the men and women who jumped out of planes to fight fires in places they couldn't reach with a vehicle.

Hammer said, "We'll get the fire turned, ma'am."

"Thank you."

He walked off with his dark-featured friend. A brooding blond guy caught up to them, completing the trio. The young one, who resembled Hammer in a way that made her wonder if they were related, reluctantly moved away from the rest of the teens, and the four strode off by themselves.

Orion watched her and Charlie rather than the kids.

He needed to get moving with his crew, and so did Charlie. She couldn't drag them into helping her any more than she already had. After all, it was the campers' job to save their academy.

Save lives.

Protect property.

The land came last—important, but not more than life or homes.

Meanwhile, Jayne stuck to the calling God had written on her heart. Teaching kids to be as safe as they could be while they dreamed of walking in these hotshot footsteps. The more training any of them got, the better, and her camp was a great way for them to see if they wanted to continue with the job—like Rumor McCabe, a smokejumper she knew. Or Logan Crawford, currently a smokejumper in Ember. Both of them had been through this program.

Like Orion, determined to be a smokejumper himself.

As much as it scared her that he wanted to jump out of planes, wasn't that what she'd taught him to do? Take the risk. Do what God had called him to do. Save lives. Fight fires.

She'd taught him to do the hard thing, even if it was scary. To put in the work because it was worth it. Like with Charlie and his kidney problems, not letting it keep him from doing what he loved to do.

The hotshot crew chief, Conner Young, slung his arm around Tiger's neck. The kid busted out laughing. Dakota had both the twins' rapt attention, telling his nephews some story.

She moved to the porch rail and watched for a while. Bridget came out of the cabin where the admin offices were and headed over.

Orion waved to her and hung the whistle around one of the kids' necks.

Smoke on the horizon wouldn't slow, even if she wanted to hit pause on all of it. The fire would come, just like danger seemed to have reached her camp. Someone else could be killed like the propane delivery driver had been.

She was going to have to face what was

happening here. Connect with the sheriff about what was going on.

Let her son live the life he wanted to live, and trust God to keep him safe.

"I have to go."

She turned and found Charlie in her space. "Please be careful."

A sad smile crossed his face. "I promise everything is going to be okay." He leaned down and kissed her cheek.

She wanted to pull him to her. Hold on while things seemed intent on changing.

I have to go.

She turned away and cupped her hands around her mouth. "Let's make these hotshots some sandwiches they can take with them."

Bridget passed her. "I'll take sandwich duty."

Jayne sniffed. She moved as fast as she could to her office without running. Door closed. Light on. She swiped at her face.

Stupid tears.

All because her life had shifted so dramatically in the last few days that she didn't know what to do. The future she'd resigned herself to meant living one summer at a time. Finding peace in the task of preparing the next generation of wildland firefighters. Trying her hardest to be content when it got lonely.

Now it was like everything she didn't have dangled in front of her.

She just had to have the courage to reach out and take it. Her life could be something beautiful rather than like a dry desert only watered by the occasional rain.

She sank into her chair and prayed Charlie had

the strength to do his job and didn't hurt too much. She prayed God would make it clear if she was supposed to take a step of faith here. That He would give her the courage to fight the fear of being denied and reach for what she wanted.

Then she rolled her chair to the cabinet and opened the rental folder for the cabin, looking for her photocopy of Roger Kirkpatrick's driver's license.

She leafed through all the pages twice just in case it had been misfiled.

But it was gone.

EIGHT

CHARLIE USED A BANDANNA TO WIPE THE SWEAT from his face. Beside him, Houston uncapped a water, drank half of it, and then poured the other half over his face and head. A couple of the guys soaked their bandannas and tied them around their necks. Sanchez had doused herself a while back, but her hair looked like it had nearly dried again since then.

Charlie picked up the chain saw and cut off a couple thicker branches that leaned out over the line. Anything they could do to widen the strip between the fire and all this dry vegetation waiting to go up in flames meant they kept fighting the good fight.

But Charlie wasn't interested in metaphors for life, even if firefighting had provided him with many over the years.

He shut off the chain saw and turned it so Hammer could grab it from him.

"Thanks." The big guy jogged away with it.

At the far end of the row of hotshots all working on their section, Orion looked to be deep in conversation with Conner Young, their boss.

Charlie headed over in time to hear Conner say,

"Any hint this thing is going sideways, and you hightail it back to the camp. Okay? I'm sure Charlie will go with you." Conner waved at him.

"You're worried?" They all were...all the time. But this one was personal. He clapped the kid on his shoulder. "We'll make sure they're safe."

Orion brushed off his hand. "We're not normally this close to camp. That's all."

"The wind?" Charlie asked.

Conner looked up at the trees. "I noticed it as well."

"Do you have an updated weather report?" Maybe Conner had information that would help Orion settle. He didn't like the idea that the kid was worried. Charlie was worried as well, about everyone at camp and the destruction that could occur there.

Only, now that he knew Orion was his son, he had that extra layer on top—being worried about Orion as well.

The whole thing was more exhausting than failing kidneys.

"There's another fire to the north, and if this one joins that, it could spell something bad for all of us," Conner said. "We need to get this line dug and then walk the north edge of the fire."

"We're done." Hammer strode up. "The boys and I will head along the north edge, do some scouting."

Conner nodded. "I want regular reports."

"Yes, sir." Hammer jogged away to Kane, Saxon, and Mack. They almost seemed like they were operating some kind of protective detail over Sanchez. Then other times, they left her and went off to do their own thing.

Charlie said, "I'll get back to digging in." He

93

wanted Orion to go with him, but the kid chose the far end of the line. Charlie had Houston right beside him again. "Any advice on what I do with that?"

"It's been a lot." Houston grabbed a spare shovel and started getting loose dirt on the flames closest to them, suffocating the smoldering brush so it died out. "Is it any wonder he needs some time to process?"

Charlie dug beside his friend. "What if we don't have that much time?"

"It has been a busy season so far. But what do I know about what 'normal' is for wildland firefighting, or firefighting at all?" Houston grinned. "I'm a pastor."

"Turns out you're good at both things." Charlie tossed another shovelful of dirt.

"You and Orion...same thing. You don't know what normal is going to look like. All you have is this first glimpse of what your father-and-son thing is going to be like. You've hit the ground running in the middle of a crisis, with no idea what normal is."

"Survival mode."

"Kind of." Houston nodded. "If you live in crisis, you can't understand normal. Your body gets accustomed to the stress, and then when it's time to rest or even calm yourself, your systems don't know how to ratchet things back down."

"Reminds me of my grandpa, and my dad."

"Veterans, weren't they?"

Charlie nodded. "Grandpa was in World War II. My dad served in Vietnam. They both had this tension...it was unreal. They could react so fast it was like they flinched before the thing startled them. They both had issues acclimating to civilian life. They just dealt with it in different ways. Grandpa went to church. Dad spent every night at the bar."

"It's tough when you don't have a good legacy to draw from." Houston rolled his shoulders. "All we can do is ask God for wisdom, which it turns out is more than enough of what we need. God knows you don't have any idea how to help Orion or even connect with him. He knows what the fire will do today. He knows how things will turn out. *He knows.*"

Charlie kicked the shovel deep with his boot. He hadn't even thought about God knowing everything about his medical situation and his plan, plus how it would all turn out at the end of the summer.

There was comfort in the fact He saw it all—past, present, and future.

Grandpa said You had the whole world in Your hands.

Charlie had believed that as a kid, but it seemed like in becoming an adult and realizing he was more like his father than anyone else, he'd lost his grip on faith. He'd barely tried to fight against the steady drift away from what he'd been taught at church.

After Grandpa died, the day before he turned thirteen, he'd figured... What was the point? Charlie had proved his dad right and managed to disappoint him at the same time he got his attention off the bar for a while.

So what if it got him a juvie record in the process?

Fire camp had been his dad's last-ditch effort to get him on some kind of straight and narrow—or just get rid of him for the summer.

It turned out Charlie loved firefighting. It got under his skin and drove him in a way nothing else had. He'd lived and breathed being a first responder for years—for himself and for the people he wanted to be proud of him.

For his grandpa.

Jayne headed back to the main house, watching the smoke on the horizon. Closer than it had been when she'd left to walk a few kids down to the propane truck. The fire was closing in. The propane truck was still overturned, blocking the road. Three of the kids' parents had opted to drive as far as they could and pick up their kids to take them home until the danger to the camp passed.

The rest of the kids either wanted to stay, or their parents didn't care what they did or were unavailable on vacation or whatever. Aria's parents were out of contact. Tiger's and the Masterson twins' parents knew that being smart kept you safe in a dangerous situation. They were making their way here, but it would take a day or two.

Alexis didn't need to be alone in a motel in Ember.

All of them wanted to help fight the fire and keep the camp safe anyway. This was what she'd been teaching them all summer.

Right now she had them eating lunch while she took the others to meet their folks. After the breakfast they'd had, she wasn't all that hungry, but she grabbed a water bottle and went to check her messages in the office. Bridget had a training video for them to watch this afternoon followed by study time for an assessment that got them through this fortnight of their training.

Jayne watched them joking with each other over

sandwiches, looking for those nuances that revealed that a person felt left out or had their feelings hurt. She worked hard to get them to function as a team. Out working a fire, they'd have to rely on each other to watch their backs. That would play in if they went on to be wildland firefighters or in whatever career they chose.

Tiger sat on the end of one of the long tables, hammering away on a guitar, singing a terribly off-key tune that seemed to just be the line "Take a chance on me" over and over again. Meanwhile, one of the girls by Alexis flushed pink.

Jayne chuckled to herself over the kid and his heartbreaker antics as she wandered down to her office to check her messages. Hopefully the sheriff had called her back. She knew he had his hands full, but there had been a gunman up here earlier in the day. The kids had played it off as a hunter or someone that'd run off as fast as they'd come, but she saw the fear in some of their eyes—mostly the ones who headed home.

A dark-haired man stood in her office, peering out the window.

"Can I—"

He turned.

"Roger." So many questions rolled through her mind. "Did you hear the gunshots earlier?"

He eased away from the window, holding his arm close to his side.

She frowned. "What's going on?"

The guy was late thirties, but she got a brother vibe from him. Maybe just because he seemed respectful. Of her time and her personal space.

He had dark hair, hazel eyes, and a bump on his

nose. He'd shaved since she saw him last, and it had grown back so that the lower half of his face was covered with stubble. A good guy, but with a dark side—a dangerous edge she hadn't seen but could very well imagine.

"Why don't you sit?"

He eased into her chair with a groan.

"What happened?"

"Doesn't matter. I got away."

She didn't see any blood, but he might've bandaged whatever it was. "Do you need medical attention? I have staff who know what they're doing, and a few of my kids have some emergency medical training."

He shook his head. "I wrapped it."

"What's going on, Roger?"

He winced. "That was a fake ID. Can you do me a favor and not tell the sheriff that I'm hanging around up here?"

"No, I'm afraid I can't do that when lying to him could put the kids in danger." They were already in enough danger with the threat of the fire. But then, it could turn and head away from them just as easily as it came near.

There was often little margin between salvation and destruction.

Until the aftermath.

"I guess that's fair."

Why had he come here? "If that was you this morning, who was the other guy?"

"His name is Earl. He's a very dangerous man. If you see him, run."

"Is he gone?" *Please tell me he's far from here now.* She needed a copy of that picture Charlie had shown her so she'd know who to avoid—and be able to give the kids the same instructions.

Thankfully they'd all be inside this afternoon. She would worry if they were out in the woods working the fire until they all knew for sure that this Earl guy was gone.

Roger shook his head. "I lost him. That's when I fell. He's probably doubled back by now, still searching for me."

"So in order to be safe, you hide here with innocent people?"

"Another fair point. Sorry I'm putting you all in danger, but in my defense, I don't plan on being here much longer."

As if him leaving made anything better. She had to fight the need to draw in people who needed protection. Instead, it was up to Roger—or whatever his real name was—to take care of himself. "Don't get caught in the fire on your way out. Take the road back to town. Go see the sheriff."

He winced. "That's how you all got stuck here, because that truck exploded."

"The land mines were because of you?" A man had died.

"I came to say thanks for everything."

Jayne frowned.

"You've been amazing. You gave me a place to stay when I desperately needed it, but you're right. For the same reason I didn't stay with my family. I didn't want to put them in danger. I don't want to do that with these kids either."

"I appreciate that." She wanted to know what she could do to help him, though. "Do you need an ATV?"

He smiled. "In a rush to see me gone?"

"Seems like it would be easier to dodge bullets if you're moving faster."

He chuckled, groaned, and chuckled some more. "I have a friend who used to say the same thing. Told the craziest stories. You never believed they were true. Now it's like my whole life is a crazy story." He eased up out of the chair. "Thank you, Jayne. For everything."

She wasn't sure she'd done all that much. "You're welcome." Not wanting to leave it like this, she said, "Is there anything I can do?"

He stopped at the door. "Just keep these kids safe."

"I plan on it. Take care."

Commotion erupted in the dining hall. She went to see what it was and didn't spot Roger in either direction.

He must've ducked out the side exit, drawing a dangerous man away from camp.

Be that as it may, she was still going to tell the sheriff that Earl guy was up here, near her kids.

The police weren't going to tromp through a wildfire to find a dangerous man, but they could at least check that her place was safe.

Jayne said, "What is it?"

Alexis turned back, already at the door. The rest of the kids were on the porch. "Smokejumpers!"

She went and gathered with them on the gravel in front of the main house, watching the plane circle. Every couple of seconds, a body left the plane, falling through the sky before the parachute caught them and they started to descend more slowly.

Eight in total.

Her heart lodged in her throat every time. "And Orion wants to do that."

One of the twins, Samuel, turned. "Of course! It's epic."

Jayne grinned. "I suppose it is." If you weren't a mother watching your son fall out of a plane on purpose.

Alexis eyed her. "He wants to save lives. And smokejumpers are, like, the *elite* of wildland firefighters."

The implication being that was the man Jayne had raised. She pulled Alexis to her side, hugging the girl. Something she normally wouldn't do with a camper— but this was her son's half-sister, and the girl was without a mother.

"See." Alexis waved up at the smokejumpers. "They all made it out fine."

Tiger said, "It's not the fall that kills you. It's the part where you hit the ground."

Jayne gaped.

Alexis busted out laughing.

The Masterson twins both whacked Tiger on the back of the head. "Bro. Not cool."

Jayne said, "All right. Once they're out of sight, everyone get back inside. We have class."

They filed by her into the building. Jayne hung around a little longer, watching the smoke cloud. The windsock on top of her cabin blew straight out, but the tip dropped at the end. So about fifteen mph wind speed.

Driving the wildfire right to their doorstep.

But with the threat of a dangerous man in the area, she wasn't sure which to worry about more.

NINE

"Thanks for letting me come with you."

Orion kept walking along the trail, ahead of Charlie. "Free country."

"Is that really the reason why you didn't object?" Charlie scanned the forest—void of animals, who had moved on to safer areas. Smoke hung in the air. They'd seen the smokejumper team land hours ago and finished up their day of work. The bus had picked up the rest of the crew—taking them back to the Ember base camp for the night.

Another day done. No lives lost, and no property destroyed by fire.

Something to celebrate.

Only God knew what tomorrow would bring. Certainly the weatherman didn't.

"It's not exactly complicated figuring why you'd want to go to the fire camp for the night."

Charlie couldn't tell if the kid was mad or bitter or what. "Keep talking. Tell me what's going on."

"Couple days, you're already moving in."

"You think I'm trying to start something with your mom?"

"Why wouldn't you? She's great."

Charlie didn't think Orion saw that as a good thing. "Because you saw me kiss her cheek this morning when we left, or what?"

Orion said, "You tell me."

They'd reached the lake, which meant it wasn't far to the camp. Clouds stacked up above the mountains to the west, huge expanses of smoke high in the sky. Ash fell to the ground around them. Charlie saw a shed. "What's in there?"

It would make a terrible shelter, but it was the only thing out here. If it came down to making a run for it and they had to flee camp, the lake was their best shot. A helicopter could land on the beach and rescue the campers.

"Bunch of canoes. You gonna take my mom out on the lake? Get her to kiss you under the stars?"

Charlie said, "Is your mom's love life really any of your business? She's an adult, and so are you. Pretty sure you don't get a say until maybe something permanent happens."

Charlie might not be around for that, and he wouldn't want to see her marry some other guy anyway, but he didn't want Orion getting all tangled in knots over his mom falling in love.

"I do if she's making another mistake."

"There's nothing about you that was a mistake." Charlie couldn't believe the kid would even think that. "Maybe not the wisest choice, but who you are is up to you and not the decisions your mom and I made. Not at this point in your life."

"So tell her to be happy for me." Orion glanced back. "I wanna be a smokejumper next year. I need her blessing."

"Do you?"

"I want it."

"Okay." Charlie nodded. "I'll help her work through it so she can be happy for you."

Orion eyed him, like he hadn't been sure it would be that simple. Then they were at the camp, so there was nothing else to say that the others wouldn't hear.

Bridget, the older woman who worked here, came out of the main building. "Did you see Sparky on your way in?"

Orion shook his head.

"Who?" Charlie didn't know who they were talking about.

"The dog. I'll get him, Bridget." Orion wandered toward another building. "Sparky! Where you at, boy! Sparky!"

Bridget said, "The dog will come for Orion, even when he's scared. I just hope he isn't hurt." She shook off the worry and said, "Jayne is inside. The kids should be about done with dinner prep."

"Thanks."

"Alexis passed her phase four written test." Bridget smiled. "All the kids did, but you should be very proud of her."

"I am." Charlie nodded.

"She'll make a wonderful RN or paramedic, or even a firefighter, if that's what she decides to do." Bridget patted his arm and wandered off after Orion.

Charlie hung his head. She would be wonderful, but he wasn't going to be around to see what Alexis became. No matter how much he might want to fight to live, it wasn't just him that would have to pay the price. It would cost Alexis. Maybe even Jayne, and Orion for sure.

Three of them. Where before it had been just his daughter — and that was bad enough.

Why did You make this harder? Aren't You supposed to lighten a man's burdens?

The sound of a small engine approached from down the dirt road. A second later, an ATV came into view. On top of it, a man in uniform. The local sheriff.

He pulled all the way up in front of the main house, and Charlie went to meet him. "Hutchinson, right?"

The sheriff nodded.

"I'm Charlie Benning. You've been talking with my teammate Dakota about finding Earl?"

The sheriff nodded again, a pinched expression on his face. Did he think Dakota should stay in his lane? Charlie wasn't sure what lane an ex-SWAT officer who'd been through rehab for a pain pill addiction and then chose to be a hotshot was supposed to be in. Dakota's instincts were all cop, born of years of training and work. He wasn't going to let a murderer go free.

Considering he'd seen this Earl guy up here just yesterday, he was inclined to agree with Dakota on this one. The guy needed to be caught.

Jayne came outside, wiping her hands on a dish towel. "Sheriff." They shook.

"Sounds like you've had a full few days."

Jayne nodded. "Any update on clearing the road? That truck is blocking us from evacuating."

"I spoke to the BLM. They're not worried that the fire will reach the camp, but they did put a rush on that wrecker. We'll clear your road soon."

Charlie said, "Maybe you could have the BLM

talk to Miles Dafoe. He's not quite as convinced the camp is safe."

"That why you're here?"

He didn't want to fully answer the sheriff's question. Not when Orion had also grilled him on his intentions toward Jayne. Couldn't he just live each day as it came without working an angle? Houston had told him to trust God. To rest in Him and quit living in survival mode—which was difficult when his days were numbered down to just a few weeks.

Sooner or later, he wouldn't have any left.

Most people didn't know when they were going to die, they didn't get to enjoy their last days like Charlie could. If people would quit hounding him, anyway.

"Why don't you tell us why you've paid us a visit, Sheriff?" Jayne held the dish towel on her hip. "Did you finally get my message that the man you're looking for was seen up here?"

Sheriff Hutchinson scratched at his jaw. "I'd like to take a look around, if that's all right. Make sure he's not tucked away somewhere."

"Be my guest."

"I've got my men spread thin, working on evacuating folks that live between here and Snowhaven."

The town to the southwest lay in the path of the part of the fire that had branched off. No one wanted to endanger an entire town by routing the fire that way. The wind, however, might have different ideas.

"I'd also like to see if your guest is still here."

"He told me he was moving on, to keep us safe."

Charlie turned to face Jayne. "You saw him?"

She nodded, a look on her face like *I'll tell you later.* "He was concerned he'd put us in danger."

"Did he tell you his real name?" the sheriff asked. When Jayne shook her head, he said, "I believe it's actually Crispin Lamb. I showed the copy of his picture that you sent me to Sophie—she confirmed it is him."

"Who is Sophie's brother?" Charlie couldn't figure how the guy might fit in with Earl the murderer and the guy he'd killed—who turned out to be some kind of secret agent, for the good guys or the bad guys.

"That's what I'm attempting to figure out," the sheriff said. "She doesn't know where he's been for six years or why he's here now. If Earl is up here looking for him, then Crispin is tied into something. Earl and his brother Floyd—they set their minds to something and they chase it down. They don't let anything get in their way."

Jayne glanced at Charlie. "I don't like the sound of that."

"I just wish I knew what got a bee in their bonnets this time."

"At least they might have moved on." Charlie shrugged. "But we'll be keeping an eye out."

The sheriff nodded. "Take care. I'll let y'all know when I leave."

Jayne set her plate on the tiny porch table. Charlie laid his on top. They both sat back in their chairs. Bridget had volunteered to sit with the kids for dinner—not that they needed more than general supervision. Though, Jayne planned to talk to each one before bedtime and make sure they were doing all right with the situation. Bridget had shoved Jayne and Charlie out to sit on the porch and eat where it was quiet.

Charlie said, "Nice night."

She stared at the glow on the horizon above the trees. Lower than it had been, since the fire shrank back in the cooler night temps. "It always is. Summer glows at night. Fall is amazing, all orange and brown. In winter everything is under snow, and it's so beautiful. There's this thing called a hoar frost, and it's like all the branches are covered in crystals. In the spring everything thaws, and all you can see is green everywhere. Bunny rabbits hopping around. Deer and elk. Bears."

He was staring at her.

"What?"

"You love it here."

"I've never wanted to be anywhere else." She sighed, the kind of tired that came after a long day of work. Some stress that wasn't normal, but in general, the day had been as normal as she could make it. "Maybe at first that was because my mom kicked me out. The camp director—you remember Mr. Halpert?" When he nodded, she said, "He's the one who found me walking on the side of the highway with my backpack."

"I wish I could thank him for helping you when you had no one."

"Mr. Halpert and his wife had me deep dive into a Bible study and really seek the Lord for what the future was going to bring. They said not to call you while I was still emotional. That it should be a rational decision that was important but not as emotionally charged as it would be in the heat of the moment. Telling you that I was pregnant."

She was aware of Charlie turning to look at her.

She couldn't face him, but she did need to get this out. "I think maybe I got too comfortable here. I liked where I was, helping out through the winter. A search and rescue training group came through, and I was only doing housekeeping type stuff, but I got to talk with them. It was really interesting, and it felt like I was helping them do their work. Even that little bit.

"I wanted to call you. So many times. I think I got too used to what I had. I didn't want anything to change." She swallowed. "I was scared. Like when I was told my dad had died. When I realized my mother was only going to withdraw and never let the wound heal. Scared down to my soul, in a way that felt like being paralyzed."

Charlie reached over and intertwined his fingers with hers.

"Do you think you can ever forgive me?"

His fingers tightened around hers, barely a reflex. "Jayne—"

The front door flung open so hard the screen snapped back on its hinges. Orion strode across the porch and down the steps, chased by the camp dog. It hadn't taken him long to find the dog earlier, spooked by something and hiding in the fire gear shed. Crazy dog liked the smell of sweat—probably a jacket or shirt Orion had worn once.

Their son didn't even look back at them.

"Something I should know?"

Charlie huffed, still holding her hand. "He's assuming I'm here to make a move on you. Like that would be my agenda."

"Holding hands probably isn't convincing him otherwise. But it's nice, and I'd prefer if you didn't let go." She hated the idea of that paralyzing fear creeping up on her again. Having Charlie with her helped more than she'd have thought possible.

Orion disappeared around one of the buildings. Probably headed to the patch of grass they kept mowed by the entrance. He liked to throw a ball for Sparky before they headed to bed, where the dog would lie on his feet all night.

"He wanted to take that dog to the Ember base camp. Sparky is a stray who wandered into camp a few years ago with no collar. We took pictures and posted them on the local community pages, but no one claimed him, so Orion kept him. But when he went to put Sparky in his truck, the dog flat out refused. He was scared to ride in a vehicle."

"That's odd."

She'd thought so too at the time. "He's happy here, and Orion usually visits when he can, so they see each other."

"He's a good man."

She sighed. "When the fire season ends, he spends four months pushing snow—he has a snowplow attachment for his truck. Spring, he landscapes. All of it is so he can return to firefighting come summer. And become a smokejumper." The last part was hard to say.

Charlie lifted her hand and pressed a kiss to the back of it. "There are never any guarantees. Not for any of us."

"I should know how to trust God better than this." She bit her lip. "Maybe I'm just too selfish. Maybe I raised a selfish son who can't watch his mom date anyone."

"Or he's used to being the man in your life, and things are changing. For both of you."

"Or he's thrown by the whole thing because I've never dated much. Plus it's *you*." Maybe Orion thought she'd been pining for Charlie all these years—which meant her son hadn't been enough to fill her heart.

"It is me." Charlie chuckled. "I mostly just dated moms of kids who were in school with Alexis. Then I'd get invited to sports events and other stuff where Alexis might be. I got to see her play basketball and softball."

Jayne loved that he'd sought out his daughter. They'd both made so many mistakes, but this was where God had them right now. "She's a great kid."

"I can't take any credit for that."

"You had more of an impact than you know, I think." Wasn't that true of anyone? People never even saw the extent of the reach they had—the lives they touched either directly or inadvertently.

Like something as simple as the letter Charlie carried. The one addressed to her.

She wanted to ask him about it, but once again, that paralyzing fear crept in like a cold front turning everything to stone the way ice did.

With the kids, she could be courageous, encouraging, and the mentor they needed. When her heart got involved, fear overtook everything and she couldn't move. Couldn't speak.

The dog yelped from across the camp.

Jayne stood up so she could lean on the porch rail and look out. Sparky raced around the corner of the building closest to the entrance, running at full speed. "Sparky, come!"

The dog raced to the door, which opened as Alexis came out. "Whoa, Sparky." The dog raced past her, nearly knocking her over, and into the building. "What's going on?"

"I don't know." Jayne headed down the steps.

"Orion was with the dog." Charlie followed her.

Alexis came with them. "Where?"

"Over by the entrance." Jayne started walking faster. The kids all knew about Earl, and she'd shown them his picture. They weren't allowed outside without someone with them—and not after dark at all.

She glanced back and saw they'd been followed by both Shellys, Tiger, and the local boy, Niall. Tiger had a flashlight, and Niall carried a baseball bat. She didn't like the look of that, but they all wanted to pitch in for her son. Who could argue with teens that cared?

Jayne reached the grassy area they called "the meadow" first. "Everyone fan out and look for Orion." Above her in the sky, she spotted the constellation he was named after. The one she and Charlie had found, stretched out on the grass. The only one they'd known the name of—something that had made them laugh.

Lord, help us find him, please.

The kids spread out. Alexis walked beside her, holding a flashlight of her own, scanning the ground.

Where was he?

"What's over there?" Charlie called out, pointing. The only one not familiar with the area.

"The river."

Tiger said, "We should go check. He might've fallen down."

Jayne headed that direction. "There are a couple of spots that are pretty steep. But he knows this area like he knows his truck." Why would he have fallen?

A smaller hand clasped hers. Jayne and Alexis jogged to the edge, where Tiger had his flashlight pointed down. "I see him."

Charlie stalled the kid with a hand on his chest. "We need ropes. No one goes down there without my say so."

Jayne crouched at the edge of the muddy bank that dropped ten or so feet down a steep incline to the rushing ice-cold river—snow runoff that led to the lake. She could make out Orion's shoulder, his body facing away from them. The rest of him was obscured by brush.

Not moving.

She gasped. "Orion!"

TEN

"HOLD."

From up the hill, Samuel—the older twin nephew of Dakota—said, "Holding."

Charlie found his footing on the loose dirt and rocks, secured by a rope back up to the top of the hill. "Orion?" He shifted his weight and got the webbing ready to haul his son up the little hill. Had he hit his head? Been hurt worse than that?

Orion lay curled away from him, a knot on the back of his head. Charlie patted his shoulder. "You awake?"

He tried to keep his tone light, but it didn't work.

"Is he conscious?" Jayne called down from the top, worry putting that quiver in her tone.

Orion moaned but didn't rouse.

"Let's get him up." Charlie wrestled the webbing around his son and hauled him up under his arms. "Okay, bring us up."

The teens on the rope up the hill started to pull back, which gave Charlie the momentum to take a step. Holding Orion like this wasn't easy. Not that

114

he'd let on how much it took out of him to haul a guy who probably weighed about the same as he did.

They trudged up the hill, Charlie doing all the stepping. Until halfway up, when Orion moaned aloud and grasped at him. "Hold!"

The teens stopped pulling.

"Orion." Charlie shifted his son in his arms. Orion got his feet under him. "Don't back up. We're clipped together."

Orion blew out a long breath.

"And we're walking." Charlie called out, "Okay, bring us up."

They reached the top of the hill, and the kids unhooked Orion from him and laid Charlie on the ground. Charlie stepped out of the harness, and Jayne slammed against him. The hug was brief, just a relieved squeeze and a nose full of the scent of her shampoo. Then she went to kneel by Orion.

Alexis crouched, and they all looked Orion over.

The hotshot shifted on the ground and lifted a hand to shield his eyes from the glare of the flashlights. "I'm good."

"We'll see about that." Jayne shifted from her knees to a crouch. "Let's get you inside and we can take a look at you."

She directed the teens to help Orion stand, and the twins got under his arms to help him walk to the main house—though it did seem like Orion did most of the walking himself.

Charlie put his arm around Alexis's shoulders. "I'll need help too."

He tugged her to his side.

She chuckled. "Right. What about rescuer safety?

You shouldn't have gotten hurt just now. You should be able to walk on your own."

Jayne got under his left arm and held his wrist over her shoulder. "We all need support sometimes."

They walked together like that after the rest. Charlie sank into the feel of his two girls—his arms around them. Holding them close.

"That was a pretty great rescue." Alexis sounded almost nervous.

"I've done ones that were a lot worse and ones that were little things. You never know, when you go into the firehouse, what a shift is going to be like."

Jayne said, "At least out here we have the weather report and the fire forecast. I'd rather be prepared and see it coming."

"That's why you've got to be prepared for anything."

Alexis squeezed his waist, which hurt his back more than he'd let her know. "You can't possibly be prepared for anything."

"I can try." Just like with the plan. "Like making sure everyone around me is going to get through it if things go wrong."

"So you take the danger just to safeguard others?"

"Some rescues don't need more than one person. If anyone else had come down with me to get Orion, it could've made it more complicated, which opens you up for more chance something could go wrong." But that wasn't what he'd been talking about. "I put my life on the line every day, but I do it knowing that you're going to be okay no matter what happens to me."

They stopped on the porch, and she turned to him. "You think there's a chance in this world that I'll be okay if something happens to you?" Her eyes filled with tears.

He touched her cheek. "I guess not. But I can be certain there will be people around to support you."

"And that's going to take the place of having a father?"

Maybe they had no choice. "We can't change what might happen. Sometimes you do everything you can, and things still go wrong."

Alexis lifted her chin. "Would you give up firefighting if I asked you?"

"That might not be enough to keep me alive," he said. "But I'm not going to be a burden on you, Lexi. I'm going to make your life good—the way I should've been able to all along. I'm going to give you what I was never able to."

"What's wrong with you?"

Jayne touched his arm.

Alexis said, "And don't tell me everything is going to be okay. I know you. There's something wrong."

A tear slipped from the corner of his eye. "I'm not going to be a burden."

"Guys." Tiger appeared at the open door. "Oops. Sorry to interrupt, but Orion is asking for all of you."

Alexis said, "This conversation isn't finished," then turned and strode inside.

Jayne slid her hand down his arm to clasp his fingers. "You need to tell her you're going to fight this illness with everything you have."

Charlie looked at her. "Being here with you makes me want to."

He let go of her hand and followed Alexis. The teens had crowded around Orion, who lay on the couch in front of the TV. He looked exasperated more than anything, but when he saw Charlie, he lifted his chin. "Thanks."

Charlie nodded, too choked up by everything to speak.

"Okay, let's give Orion some space." Jayne cleared out the kids, and Bridget shone a tiny flashlight in Orion's eyes.

"I don't see any indication of a concussion," Bridget said. "Any injuries?"

"Just bruises." Orion shifted and grabbed his opposite arm, then rolled his shoulders. "I landed funny, but I'll be all right."

Charlie said, "Don't worry. No one is gonna sideline you from firefighting. But you did get knocked out."

"Only for a few minutes, right? I just have a headache."

Alexis had left with the kids, so it was just him and Jayne, Bridget, and Orion.

Bridget sank into the armchair. "You should still see a doctor. When you can get to one."

Orion nodded. "Sure thing."

"At least we can get a helicopter out here to pick someone up if there is an emergency."

Jayne nodded. "Or get the victim to the road for a pickup."

Charlie didn't like either option, since it meant someone was hurt more than a minor injury. "What happened?"

Orion bent and unlaced his boots, pulling them off one at a time.

Charlie said, "It's important."

"I know." Orion sat back, leaning his head against

the couch. "I just feel dumb. He snuck up on me, whoever he was. Shoved me. I felt the guy, then I smelled him." Orion wrinkled his nose. "Then I was falling."

That explained why the dog had run back to the house. The animal hopped onto the couch and put his head in Orion's lap.

"So you didn't see the guy?" Charlie said, "Could you describe anything about him?"

"He was bigger than me." Orion shrugged.

That ruled out "Roger"—Sophie's brother Crispin. Did that mean it was the ponytail guy, their murderer at large, Earl? Or someone connected to Earl? "Did he say anything?"

"Nope." Orion closed his eyes. "Maybe he was as surprised as I was."

Bridget got up. "I'll check on the kids."

"I need to do the same. Make sure they're all good." Jayne squeezed Orion's shoulder over the back of the couch.

Charlie watched her walk away. Her son had been in danger, and she'd weathered it. Kind of like the way she weathered the threat of the fire.

He watched her go. "She didn't lose her cool. She was worried, but it seems like that might've been good practice for her. With you potentially being in danger."

"You mean with smokejumping?"

Charlie shrugged.

"I doubt she'll ever be okay with it since it's how her father died."

"History doesn't always have to repeat itself." He eased into the chair Bridget had vacated. Alexis had asked, and he'd told her he wasn't going to be a burden. "And whether you become a smokejumper or not, I'll always be proud of who you are."

And not one ounce of it was because of him.

"Thanks…Dad." Orion pushed out a breath.

Charlie had to sniff. "Will you take care of Alexis and your mom?"

Orion frowned.

"Just in case anything happens to me."

The minute he told them what was really going on, both Orion and Alexis would want him to do whatever it took to live. That just wasn't an option. No matter how much it made his heart squeeze in his chest to even think about what he'd be leaving behind now.

It had been almost unbearable when it was just Alexis. Now it was Jayne and his son as well.

"If you do the same," Orion said. "Just in case."

Charlie nodded, choking out the word "Deal."

Orion held out his hand. Charlie clasped it. His son said, "God brought you here this summer for a reason, and I'm glad He did."

Charlie squeezed Orion's hand.

Before he could say anything, screaming erupted in the hallway.

Jayne took a half step back, then surged toward the two girls who had launched at each other in the middle of a spat that had turned physical. "Both of you back off."

She got between them—Shelly from California, and Aria, who Alexis knew from Last Chance County. They'd been roommates all summer but barely talked to each other outside of the time they shared that space. When Jayne had knocked on their door, she hadn't thought she would find this.

All she could do was thank God she'd discovered it before it got much worse.

Shelly cried, one hand on her cheek. "She slapped me."

Jayne wasn't going to point out that from her vantage point it had looked like Shelly had started the entire thing. "One of you tell me what's going on."

Aria fisted her hands by her sides, her face red. "She said my parents obviously don't care about me since I haven't been able to get ahold of them. But the team has gone radio silent. There are rules."

Aria wasn't going to say *Chevalier Protection Specialists* aloud, but Jayne had all the information on the kids who applied here.

Shelly wailed. "She didn't need to slap me!"

Jayne said, "Go get some ice or a cold washcloth for your face." She watched Shelly leave and spotted Charlie at the door, concern written on his face. "Aria, what would your mom and dad say about you slapping someone?"

"If they deserved it?" She sank onto the edge of the bed. "You don't want to know. But I get what you mean."

"You haven't been able to reach them?"

Aria shook her head, her straight black hair swinging side to side.

"I can call the number in your file, but I don't recall getting a reply to my emails."

"Aria Hondo, right?" Charlie leaned against the doorframe. Right now he looked as calm as he had bringing Orion up from the riverbank. How did he do

121

that? The focus seemed to give him the ability to push everything else out and give whatever was in front of him his full attention.

Was it wrong that she adored when it was directed at her?

"You're from Last Chance County?" He paused. "Your parents are Eas and Karina?"

Jayne frowned. "You know them?"

Charlie said, "You think your mom went with them on a mission?"

Jayne had no idea what they were talking about.

"Mom is at home with the baby." Aria bit her lip. "I should be able to reach her. But she hasn't called me back since yesterday."

"You want me to see who I can rouse at Chevalier?"

Jayne had heard of that group from the male campers, and all of them had awe in their tones when they discussed the team of protection specialists. Almost like they wanted to get in trouble on purpose, all so they could be rescued. She hadn't realized Aria's parents were part of the team, but if it was based in Last Chance County, it made sense that Charlie knew them.

Aria said, "Can we call Conroy and ask him to send someone to check on the house?"

"Let's do it." Charlie waved her out of the room. "Chief Barnes loves to visit folks and make sure they're all right."

Aria trailed out of the room.

Shelly wandered back from the kitchen with a washcloth pressed to her cheek. She lifted her chin as Charlie and Aria passed her, went into her room, and slammed the door shut. *Okay, then.*

Alexis rolled her eyes. Her roommate, Shelly from Alaska, was already asleep.

"You good?"

Alexis shrugged. "Everyone I care about is here and alive."

The door to the lower level swung open, and Samuel came out first, followed by his brother and Tiger, then Niall and Pablo — Mr. Romance.

Alexis came with her to stand with them at the end of the girls' hall. She also knew Pablo from Last Chance County, some EMT or firefighter's little brother, but didn't talk much with him.

Samuel said, "We wanna help fight the fire tomorrow."

"We know it's gonna be bad," his twin, Joshua, said. "That's why we want to help."

Tiger said, "Isn't that what you trained us to do?"

Alexis was the one who said, "Fighting fires is dangerous. It's not like training."

Pablo folded his arms, showing off his use of the weight bench downstairs. "We can handle it."

Alexis sighed. She turned to Jayne. "I'm going to bed. Good luck."

Jayne coughed so she didn't laugh aloud. The kids were a team when they wanted to be, but the natural divide between guys and girls became clear in moments like this.

She faced the boys. Practically men, but not adults. Yet. "I know you all want to help out."

"We listened to the weather report," Samuel said. "We know it's going to be bad tomorrow. And on the scanner we heard Miles call the smokejumpers back in for the day. He said they're deploying here tomorrow to help us."

"That's good."

"So we can go with them and help."

Jayne stared down five teen boys. In some cultures they'd be considered full-grown, but they weren't all adults. She had to balance what they believed they could do, their natural exuberance, and the liability of putting minors in danger.

In the end, she said, "I'll think about it." And pray about it. "I don't like putting any of you in danger, but that might be the reality of our situation tomorrow if things get bad."

Samuel and Joshua both nodded. Pablo shifted, about to say something. Tiger shoved him back. "Thanks, Jayne. We appreciate it."

They all disappeared back downstairs.

Jayne blew out a breath.

Aria appeared again. "The police chief in Last Chance County is gonna call my phone. He's going to my house, but he said he saw my mom at the coffee shop in town this morning with my little sister."

Jayne smiled, her attention pulled away by Charlie at the end of the hallway.

He studied her, then he waved her over. "Come here."

They were alone in the hall now. She didn't hesitate, moving all the way into his arms.

She wanted to burrow in and hide from the world—but that hadn't been a good idea when they'd done it at seventeen.

She tried to live a good Christian life these days. Not because it was what she was supposed to do, but out of respect for what God had done for her. She wasn't going to be ungrateful, but wanted to live a life honoring the choice she'd made to be a follower of Jesus.

It wasn't perfect, but it was the least she could do.

Still, the feel of his strength wrapped around her was always going to be something her heart needed. "Thanks."

He held on. "You're welcome. Looked like you needed a hug."

"I really did." She leaned back so she could look at his face. He did look a little worn at the edges. They both did these days, but he'd had a long day. "I left another message with the sheriff, but we can't actually say definitively that it was Earl up here."

"When the smokejumpers show up tomorrow, everyone gets a buddy."

"All right."

"We need a plan for if the worst should happen."

Jayne had one. "I'll walk you all through it if we can't get evacuated." She figured the call would come in first thing, and they'd be walking down the road past the propane so they could get picked up.

She would head to town with the kids. Charlie would get back to his job.

Their lives would diverge again, and they would have to put in the work to see each other. He had a medical issue that she wanted to be there for as he fought to live a long life. But Charlie lived in Last Chance County. The drive would take hours—maybe even all day. She could hardly commute back and forth from here.

"What's that look about?"

She scrunched up her nose. "Just thinking about what the future holds. Do you have doctor appointments or whatnot coming up?" Presumably with kidney failure, that meant dialysis. If she wanted to be with him, she'd have to move so she was close to where he lived—which would be close to his medical care team.

"I don't know yet how it will all go down."

"Did they give you a treatment plan?" She frowned. "Do you need a kidney transplant?"

Charlie flinched. "I'm not taking anything from anyone."

She stepped back. "If you need a kidney to save your life, what else can you do?"

He shook his head. "I'm not taking one."

"So you'd let yourself die rather than admit you need help?"

"That's not what this is."

She stared at him. "Doesn't seem like that to me. Seems like you think you know better than medical professionals."

Charlie shushed her, pulling her out into the hall. "Alexis doesn't need to know. Okay? I don't want her to worry."

Jayne gaped. "You might die, and you haven't told her."

ELEVEN

Things hadn't gone so well after that bombshell had dropped last night. Charlie had no clue how to explain it, and Jayne hadn't been interested in hearing his answer anyway.

To be fair, they were both running on empty.

Even after a night of sleep, he didn't feel much better. Bridget had made pancakes for the kids. Charlie just took a cup of coffee onto the porch and checked all the morning updates on his phone.

The wind had changed overnight. Smoke hung even thicker in the air. Miles had confirmed with him and Orion that the smokejumpers would be dropping in early.

"It's bad out here." Orion approached the porch, that mutt by his side—the one that cut and ran when things got out of control.

"You're right. It's much worse today." Charlie didn't like the way the wind blew hard and fast. "Parachuting through this will be dicey."

"Booth said they live for this stuff. All part of the rush."

"So you have a death wish?"

"Seems like I might not be the only one." Before Charlie could ask what that meant, Orion changed the subject. "I walked down to the propane truck. The fire is thick on both sides of the road. I don't think anyone will be driving up here today, even if they want to. Walking out would be risky—maybe even impossible. I don't think it's worth risking an evacuation order that will put us in more danger than staying put."

"So...what then? We wait for the wind to die down and a chopper can come in?"

Orion shrugged. The dog trotted into the house. "There's a couple spots inside to hunker down, but it won't fit all of us and the smokejumpers."

And if worst came to worst..."Everyone here has a shelter, right?"

Orion nodded. "We should do a refresher on deploying it, especially in wind, before anyone goes out."

Charlie spotted the plane and a helicopter overhead. One to carry the team and the other to get a visual on the fire and the best place for them to deploy. "Here they come."

Orion went to the door and called, "Incoming," loudly into the hall.

A thunder of feet answered, and the kids spilled out onto the gravel in front of the porch. One of the boys stared up at the sky—Joshua Masterson, Dakota's nephew. "I so wanna do that."

The first smokejumper dived out of the plane.

Charlie turned to Orion. "Does your mom know we're cut off from evacuating?"

"I do now." She stepped out onto the porch.

All the frost between them since last night hadn't

melted in the warm morning temps. Today was going to be a scorcher, but it wouldn't fix the impasse they'd found themselves at.

He just hoped she didn't say anything about it to Orion or Alexis.

"I talked to Miles on my way back up." Orion paused when one of the kids spoke.

"Let's go meet them where they land."

All the kids turned to look at their camp director.

Jayne said, "Be careful. Give them plenty of room."

The teens ran off toward the lake in a group.

Jayne said, "Did we wait here too long?"

Charlie had been thinking the same thing. "Whether we did or not, this is the situation we're in." He folded his arms, ignoring the ache in his lower back. He needed to take his morning meds but had to actually eat first. He turned to Orion. "You said you talked to Miles?"

Orion nodded. "I didn't like the look of the fire by the road out of here. He said the morning spotter called it in. They flew over and said the fire is in spots, clumps of burning trees with no fire between."

That wouldn't last long the way the wind was blowing.

Orion said, "I think someone set them on purpose. To keep us here."

"Roger—Crispin—said he was leaving. That means there would be no reason for Earl to stick around." Jayne moved to the steps and lifted her gaze to watch the last jumper.

Orion looked from his mom to Charlie. Of course the kid noticed the tension.

The last jumper deployed his parachute.

Wind whipped it violently, sending him toward them and not the lake to the west.

Charlie stepped off the porch. Jayne prayed aloud for the safety of the firefighter struggling with his toggles to control his chute.

Orion hissed a breath.

The smokejumper swung in an arc toward the cabin opposite them, hitting the crest of the roof. Charlie heard him cry out. He lowered violently to the ground in front of them, followed by the billowing chute that threatened to drag him back off his feet.

He immediately crumpled, crying out again while he disconnected the chute. It whipped up into the wind and headed for the trees with no way to retrieve it.

Tucker Newman slumped to his back with a loud groan.

Charlie reached him first, then Jayne knelt on Tucker's other side.

The smokejumper boss sat up. "Not my best entrance." His face paled. He turned to the side and threw up on the ground.

"Broken leg?" Charlie didn't like how he'd landed.

Tucker lay back on the ground with another groan. "Left." He sucked in a few breaths.

Jayne jumped up and ran to the main house.

Orion handed Charlie a multitool, the knife already extended. He cut Tucker's pant leg to his knee and winced at the look of his shin. "We need to immobilize this. Get you inside until we can get an evac."

"What happened?" Alexis raced toward them, surrounded by the other teens and smokejumpers.

Logan, Booth, Alex, Vince, Eric, and Finn—and the women, Nova and Hannah.

It looked like everyone else had made it down from the plane okay. Jayne returned with a first-aid kit. Charlie said, "We need to splint his leg."

Alexis jumped up. "I know what we can use!" She turned to one of the boys. "Get me two rolled up lake towels and some thick tape." She ran off toward the recycling trash.

"You good, boss?" Logan Crawford stepped forward.

"As long as everyone else is." Tucker grunted. "Stevie is gonna kill me when I get back to Alaska."

"We're good." That was Booth. "Glad to be here, ma'am."

"Thank you." Jayne nodded.

Alexis skidded to a stop beside him. "We can cut this." She handed over a long, skinny box with thick packaging. "Take off the front surface so we still have the back and two sides."

Tiger handed over the towels.

Alexis stuffed the box with one towel, then got the box under Tucker's leg while they held it aloft and Tucker tried not to hurl again. She padded his leg with the other towel and wrapped tape around the whole thing to hold his lower leg in place.

They lowered the limb to the ground, and Tucker groaned again.

Charlie turned to his daughter. "That was good thinking."

She flushed.

Jayne said, "Let's get him inside."

Two of the smokejumpers came forward and got

Tucker upright. The twins grabbed his knees, and they carefully carried him inside the house.

"Benning." A familiar hand clapped him on the shoulder.

Charlie spun around. "Lieutenant."

Logan Crawford held out his hand. "Ready to fight this fire?"

Tiger said, "We're gonna help."

They both ignored the kid for a second.

Charlie clasped his friend's hand and pulled him in for a brief hug. The past couple of weeks, the smokejumpers had been deploying to a different fire to the north while the hotshots had stuck closer to Ember. "Good to see you."

Jayne returned from accompanying Tucker inside. "Okay, everyone who wants to fight this fire, gear up. You buddy up with a smokejumper, or Orion or Charlie. You stay together. You come back together. You do as you're told like your life depends on it. Because it does."

The teen boys all raced inside to change and get their stuff.

Jayne addressed the rest. "If any of you are staying close to camp instead of going out, great. Let's get this place ready to withstand a fire." She said, "Logan Crawford." They shook hands. "Good to see you."

"You too, Jayne." Logan glanced at Charlie.

Booth said, "Dakota told me you guys might've seen Earl up here."

Charlie nodded. "Keep your eyes open when you're out."

Why Booth had such a vested interest in finding a gunman, Charlie didn't know. The guy's past was a mystery to all of them. Whatever he told them would probably be nothing but a fantastical story like the ones he told over the dinner table—which was where he'd heard the whole story so far from Houston and Dakota.

"If Earl is still here, then he has a death wish." Jayne folded her arms. "It's going to be up to you guys to keep this fire from destroying my entire life."

Charlie wanted to pull her into a hug, but they were surrounded by people, and it hadn't ended well last time. "Orion had a good idea. We should go over shelter deployment before we do anything."

"And cover places to shelter," Orion said. "Like the walk-in refrigerator and the basement cold storage."

"Good idea." Nova nodded. The female smokejumper—one of two on the team—always seemed ready to take charge. "Let's get everyone out here and we can have a safety briefing."

Could he get Nova and Hannah to tell Jayne all about the safety precautions they took while jumping? Maybe that would put her mind to rest about Orion doing it.

"We need to make it quick." Charlie motioned to the tree. "With the wind blowing like this, we might not have long to mount our stand."

Logan pulled his radio off his belt. "I'll get Miles to request retardant drops if he hasn't already. Let's not take any chances. No one dies today."

Jayne spun around and pinned him with a look.

Charlie winced. "If you're the kind of person who prays, now's the time to start."

It had been an hour since they'd all headed out. The kids here had deployed around the camp to assess how much time they might have. Which, if the fire started to move fast, Jayne knew full well could be a matter of a minute or two.

Fire lit the sky behind the mountains to the west, and she could see flames on the hills. Glowing spots through the hazy gray fog of smoke that indicated the fire was coming. It had stopped raining ash, which was never a good sign.

Aria had opted to stay at the main house so she could video-call her mom. The two Shellys had gone with the boys and all the smokejumpers. Orion had promised to stick with Pablo, her wildcard. Apparently Charlie worked with Pablo's brother Izan in Last Chance County. Alexis chose to go with her father.

"I think that table might be clean."

Jayne's hand ached. She let go of the washcloth and straightened to find Bridget beside her. Across the room, Tucker sat on the couch with his leg up. She'd set up a map on an easel, and he'd had Aria mark the map with the fire coverage area before she went to make her call. He was on the phone, sounding like he was coordinating with Miles. She'd tuned it out.

Hearing Orion over the radio—or any of them—that worried tone in their speech.

They had it handled.

"I guess there's no point asking if you're okay." Bridget handed Jayne a cup of coffee. "None of us are."

Jayne sipped the comforting brew and leaned against the table. "Their whole goal is to save lives, even their own. To fight the fire in such a way there's no loss of life. Then they worry about property."

She wanted to throw the cup across the room.

Bridget just waited, listening but saying nothing.

"He isn't going to fight it."

"Charlie is going to put people's lives at risk?"

Jayne shook her head. "Just his own."

He would leave her, Alexis, and Orion to deal with the aftermath. She could see plainly enough that he believed it was the right thing to do—but he wouldn't have to grieve. The pain would be over for him.

While the rest of them lived with what could've been.

"He thinks it's the best way to deal with his health issues." To die doing what he loved and leave that legacy. Maybe save someone in the process.

He would keep Alexis and Orion from having to watch him decline. Or either of them from having to live with the complications of giving their father a kidney—which would likely keep Orion from smokejumping and could prevent Alexis from having the career she wanted.

Jayne groaned. She set the coffee down on the table so hard some sloshed over onto her hand.

Ugh. Why did he have to be honorable?

Charlie was determined to make the hard choice and take the pain on himself rather than let anyone else suffer for years because of his condition.

Jayne slammed her hand on the table. "I get it. Honestly? I actually think I would do the same in his position."

She straightened and paced across the room.

Tucker stopped talking on his phone and looked at her.

She waved him off. "Ugh. I actually get it. But I don't want him to do that. It's too much to take on himself. All that responsibility? And he just wants to suffer in silence. To let us move on...without him." She let out a frustrated moan. "I'd rather have him and the hard times."

"But he thinks he's given you enough of those already."

Tears spilled from her eyes. Jayne swiped them away, angry that he got to make the decision for them all. She even understood why he wouldn't have sat them all down and explained.

He wanted to save them from even the pain of that conversation.

As much as she might want to believe it was misguided, didn't he get to choose?

Didn't she need to give him the respect of letting him make his own decision, rather than forcing him to accommodate their feelings and do what he didn't want to do?

She squeezed her eyes shut.

Bridget laid a hand on her shoulder and began to pray for wisdom. For God to move in Charlie's heart and for him to be open to listening to that still, small voice. For the protection and safety of everyone—especially the kids in this unimaginable situation.

"Amen." Jayne gave her friend a quick hug. "We need to get to work."

Bridget smiled. "The biggest problem we'll have to worry about is if the fire comes through here and the air superheats from the wind. We need to be inside under cover if that happens."

Jayne nodded. "We can get at least four in the basement storage area in a pinch. We can get eight in the walk-in refrigerator, though it's more like fifteen if we get the racks out and sacrifice the food."

"Just not the water bottles."

Even if they might need the food to keep them going, it would be tossed if it saved their lives. "But anyone else who doesn't make it inside in time will be out of luck."

By her count, between the kids, staff, and firefighters, there were at least twenty of them. Or thereabouts. They couldn't save everyone, which meant they needed a third place to hole up.

Anywhere not reinforced would burn.

Anywhere with no clean air could suffocate whoever hid inside.

Lord, help us. If the wind died down, they could get a rescue chopper in to ferry kids out. Having the smokejumpers here to help fight the fire was great for morale for the kids—but could mean someone lost their lives if they had to hide from the fire and let it blow over them.

Someone would need to deploy their shelter and ride out the heat.

If she didn't cover everyone, Charlie would give himself up to the fire. No way she was going to let that happen.

Jayne strode over to Tucker. "What's the latest?"

He adjusted his seat and winced. The painkillers they'd given him were helping but not combatting the broken leg. If they didn't get Tucker out of here, he could end up with problems that came from not being treated.

He could lose his career—or his life.

"Miles is feeding me information from the spotter planes. We have two fires converging, and they look like they're skirting toward the camp alongside the lake. I requested a water drop, but the chopper can't fly in this wind or we'd be getting rescued. They might be able to get a plane to drop more retardant, but I'm waiting for word on if it's too dangerous for them to try."

"It could be too dangerous for us if they don't."

Tucker nodded. "Miles knows that. He's getting calls from all over the country, and international numbers, asking him what he's doing to protect these kids. He's pretty sure he's got a missed call from the White House."

"These kids have connections you wouldn't believe."

Tucker said, "No one is willing to lose anyone here. Everyone is working this fire. The hotshots are to the south of us, trying to cut a line southwest to keep the fire from moving over the camp, but the embers are flying, and fires are springing up."

She tried to swallow against the lump in her throat. More people putting their lives on the line to save her and the people in her care. She loved every one of them for it, but it was the last thing she'd ever wanted to happen.

"What I'm worried about is that we have two fires colliding. With the wind, they could join forces."

"You're not talking about what I think you're talking about, are you?"

Tucker's expression darkened. "Fire tornado."

"I teach that to the kids because it's cool. Not because I think there's any chance of it actually happening." Jayne squeezed the bridge of her nose. It was an engaging lecture at the beginning of the year, a mix of weather science and crazy stories. Plus the video—trees bent nearly horizontal from the wind. Debris and embers flying.

A column of flames stretching up to the sky.

"You're telling me we could be in for a firestorm?"

Tucker nodded. "I'm afraid we have to see that as a very real possibility here."

Lord, help us.

TWELVE

THE PLANE FLEW SO HIGH CHARLIE COULD BARELY hear it over the wind. He would give the pilot, Tirzah, credit. She knew how to handle herself. Even in crazy winds like these.

The hot air blew against his face, like a fan pushing air around but giving no relief from the punishing temperatures. Trees bent over in the onslaught, branches waving like flags.

Tirzah let go of the water drop.

Moisture hit the air. She'd accounted for the wind, but the water was no match for the radiant heat from the flames. It hit the air and turned to steam before even reaching the fire.

"This isn't good." Logan had a dark expression on his face.

The rest of the smokejumpers and the firefighting teens didn't disagree. They attacked the fire with shovel after shovel overloaded with dirt. All of them were covered with sweat, ash on their faces.

Charlie inhaled but couldn't take a full breath without coughing.

Alexis came over to stand with him.

"No, this isn't good at all." They would need to get to cover if the fire kept moving like it was. It would take minutes to run to the camp. "Is the trail to the camp clear? We may need an exit strategy."

Alexis said, "I could go check it."

"Not alone." He squeezed her shoulder.

The rhythmic sound of shovels hitting the dirt, then the hiss of flames, proved almost soothing. *God, help us.*

Since he'd started praying recently, he figured he was man enough to admit they could use help. For the first time while out on a fire, he realized he wanted to be at home. In this case, that was back at the camp with Jayne.

But that wouldn't get this fire suppressed.

"We're fighting a losing battle." Orion strode over, one hand shielding his bloodshot eyes.

"But we're not giving up." They couldn't.

These kids deserved every bit of effort the adults responsible for them could muster.

"Let's get back to work."

One of the female smokejumpers got on the radio, asking for more water. Or retardant. Something. Anything.

But when would this situation turn from a rescue to a recovery?

A branch cracked.

Instinct took over. His mind barely registered the falling branch before he grabbed Alexis, spun around, and shoved her to the ground. Alexis screamed. The branch slammed into his back.

It splintered, burning his shirt against his back.

He cried out. Multiple sets of hands slammed his back, patting out flames.

"Dad."

Pain blinded him. She moved under him, and he let his arms give out so he could collapse to the ground. His face hit the dirt.

"Dad!" Orion rolled him over.

Charlie groaned.

"Hold up," someone said. "Did Orion just say 'Dad'?"

Charlie blinked. Orion grabbed his wrist and hauled him to sitting. Pain cut through him and the world spun. If Orion thought he should be sitting, it couldn't be that bad.

But Orion wasn't looking at him. He was motioning to someone else.

Cold liquid hit his back.

Charlie hissed.

"Sorry." Orion squeezed Charlie's neck.

Alexis gasped. "What's going on? I know you're not okay. Is it your back?"

Charlie gasped. "Kidneys."

Logan crouched by him. "You're gonna hurt for a while, and you'll have some blisters. Kidneys?"

Charlie nodded.

"We'll get to that." Logan frowned. "Is Orion really your son?"

Alexis crouched on Charlie's other side. "Uh, duh. It's obvious, isn't it?"

"So tell me the *not* obvious thing," Logan said. "I've worked with Charlie for years. He's never mentioned his kidneys."

"I'm fine." Charlie glanced at Alexis. He wanted to ask how she was doing, but they had a fire to fight. Later they could decompress and talk through it all—

but the truth was, he might not have a later. Not if he enacted the plan he'd come here with.

His daughter's expression hardened. "You're not fine. That makes so much sense. Your kidneys are failing, aren't they?"

"Lex—"

Orion cut him off. "What's this?"

Alexis said, "More secrets? Fantastic."

She paced away, so he couldn't see the hurt on her face. He didn't know if that was better or worse. As with figuring out his connection to Orion, she seemed to have started putting together the fact he wasn't in good health. She'd noticed his weight loss. What else had she seen?

His son stared at him. A muscle in his jaw flexed. "Does my mom know?"

The guy almost looked disappointed.

As though Charlie was worth anything.

Charlie held up both hands. "I'm not dragging everyone into this, but yes." He looked at Orion. "Your mom does know." Then he looked around. "Can we get back to fighting this fire?"

Logan got up and swiped his shovel from the ground.

Smoldering embers of the shattered branch that'd hit him littered the earth around Charlie. He wanted to sink into it and accept the exhaustion that weighed him down.

Alexis said, "You really just took that hit for me?"

"I would take all the hits for you. If I could."

She frowned. "I don't need to be babied."

"It's just me being your dad while I can." He kept his voice quiet. "With the time I have left."

Everyone else except Orion had returned to their

shoveling, which looked like it might be making progress. *Are we really going to do this?* He'd never fought such an important battle in his life.

And he wanted to win it.

Alexis said, "So you'll risk dying just to make sure I don't get hurt?"

Charlie touched her cheeks, rubbing gravel from his thumb on her chin. "Yes. Every time." After all, that was why he'd come here this summer and chosen to be a hotshot. To give his life so she didn't get hurt when everything that made up his future fractured into pieces the way her mother's had.

Orion hadn't gone anywhere. "So you're dying, but you're here fighting fires?"

Now wasn't the time for this. "I'm where I'm supposed to be."

Alexis said, "Because you're too stubborn to admit that you aren't okay."

"How I am doesn't matter," Charlie said. "What matters is that the two of you are safe and happy. That I don't take anything else from you. I've already cost you too much."

"So you'll fight this alone. Silent about what's going on." Orion pressed his lips into a thin line. "And we're supposed to say nothing? Just get on with our lives like we don't know?"

"It'll be easier...after."

Alexis flinched. "What do you..."

"After what?" Orion's brows leaned together.

"I don't want you guys to worry. I've figured it all out." Charlie didn't want to think about their family when he was gone, but this was the reality. "You'll have each other."

"But not you." Alexis paled. "You're going to let yourself die. That's what you mean, isn't it?"

He wanted to say *We can talk about it later*. But would there be a later? If he was ever going to go through with it, this storm would be the time.

"That's why you couldn't tell me what your plan was for after summer." Orion levered back on his heels and pushed up to standing. He paced away. "You're *trying* to die?"

Charlie shifted and managed to get up. Pain sliced through his back from the injury and his lower back from the situation that would take his life. He ignored both of them and faced his children. "We don't get to decide what life hands us. But I get to choose this. And it's the *right* choice for everyone."

"And we get no say?" Tears rolled down Alexis's cheeks.

The last thing he'd wanted was to cause her more hurt.

He prayed that with the wind and the noise of shovels, the others wouldn't hear.

"I can't control what's happening to me, but I refuse to take from you when I've already done that enough. It's not going to cost your futures—either of you." He glanced between them. "I won't make either of you pay this price."

"You don't get to decide that for me." Orion took a step back. "You've been my father for...what? Two days?" He turned and walked to the other end of the line.

Alexis said, "That's what you don't get."

He turned to her.

"We would all pay anything *not* to lose you." She shook her head. "But you won't even fight."

Jayne shoved back a tarp. "Fire retardant blankets. And more turnout coats, but they might have been discovered by mice, so we need to check them for holes." She lifted a stack of blankets.

Shelly from California wrinkled her nose.

"Everyone pitches in. You know that."

"I'll take these to the main house." Aria grabbed the pile from her. "You bring the rest, Shelly."

The other teen rolled her eyes at Aria's back as she headed outside. "Who died and made her the boss?"

Jayne said, "You leave a power vacuum, and someone is going to fill it. But you'd all be better off just being peers. Not rivaling for who is on top."

"Who even cares about that right now?" Shelly from Alaska grabbed an armful of turnout coats. "The fire is coming."

Then it was only Shelly from California in the storage shed with Jayne.

Perhaps fear had settled too deep below the surface. The girls had a mix of being stir-crazy and getting exhausted from all the tasks she'd occupied them with.

Maybe a movie would be a good idea while they all waited for the heat of the day to die down. That would take a few hours, and the time between now and when the fire pulled back with the cool evening temperatures could prove hair-raising.

Jayne had run them through emergency drills all morning. Everyone had talked to their parents, and Tucker had said hello to the guardians, telling them all how the teens were taking care of him.

The rest were out with the smokejumpers.

The ones at the camp would, if the order was given, help Tucker to the walk-in refrigerator and barricade the door.

Last resort, but how fast they got in there could mean the difference between life and death if the air super-heated and they really did end up with a fire tornado.

Lord, help us.

She could prepare so everyone here made it through. But what about the others?

Hot wind whipped through the open doorway.

Shelly shoved the door wide as she moved out, then ran for the main house. The girls had made a joke of racing to this shed, but Jayne wanted to check a few places before she went back to them.

She dumped a stack of turnout coats and pants outside the door and locked the building.

She stood still a moment, watching flames whip from tree to tree over by the entrance. Would they be completely encircled by fire this afternoon?

With the strength of the wind, that was a very real possibility.

The last building, over by the trail to the lake, caught her attention. Movement flashed in the window.

If an animal, or that mutt, was caught inside, she needed to let them out. Or one of the campers.

She didn't need another problem. Jayne's hands curled into fists as she tromped over to the building. The door was unlocked, for crying out loud. She shoved it open. Who had—

Roger, her guest, lay on the bare distressed-wood floor. Bloody. Rumpled. A huge bruise on the side of his face.

A punishing grip clamped down on her arm.

Jayne swallowed a cry.

The door slammed shut with her inside. She spun to see who had her in their grasp and came face-to-face with a pistol.

Dead eyes.

Dark hair with split ends hung down to his shoulders.

"What do we have here?" He yanked her around to face her guest. "Leverage." He pressed the gun against her temple. "Tell me what I want to know, or I'll blow her brains out."

Jayne sucked in a breath. There was no time for this. And no help for her if the worst happened.

Just the aftermath.

Kids in danger.

Her loved ones, grieving like she had when she'd lost her father. The way she would if Charlie had his way and succumbed to the illness ravaging him.

She wasn't going to go out without a fight.

No one should die believing that the world would be a better place without them in it. Every life was made in the image of God and valuable.

Roger—or Crispin, if this really was Sophie's brother—shifted. Pain flashed in his expression and he sat up. "Don't, Earl. There's no need to hurt her."

"Then tell me what I want to know and I won't." His grip sparked pain down to her fingertips.

"You think I won't die to protect this country from people like you?"

Earl said, "One man?" He barked a laugh. "You can hardly stop us. I'll get what I want one way or another. You can't stand in my way."

Crispin slid his back up the wall. "Let her go. This is between us."

And it was about protecting the country?

Who was this guy?

"I think she came in at just the right time."

Earl might think that, but Jayne knew he was discounting one thing. "So is the fire, by the way. So how about you two take your business elsewhere and get out of my camp."

She couldn't stand the thought that one of the kids might be in danger or hurt.

At least, not more than what they'd all been trained to handle.

Earl chuckled. "The leverage has a mouth on her."

Jayne pressed her lips together.

Crispin said, "Let her go and I'll go with you."

"Why do I need you?" Earl said. "All I need is the information. So where is it hidden?"

"Nowhere near here. You think I'd put these kids in danger?"

"Wrong answer."

Jayne didn't want to get shot. She twisted her upper body and elbowed Earl in the side as hard as she could.

He doubled over. Crispin rushed him.

The gun skittered across the floor.

Jayne dove for it.

The two men grunted behind her. She bent for the gun, and they slammed into her. Jayne's shoulder hit the wall, but she managed to keep her head from doing the same.

Crispin did some martial arts move, his arm around Earl's throat long enough that Earl's eyes fluttered closed and he slumped to the ground.

Crispin let go.

Earl launched up like he hadn't been passed out at all and slammed into Jayne.

Crispin raced after him out the door.

Jayne stumbled to it and looked out in time to see them both disappear into the woods.

She still had the gun.

She sprinted for the main house, up the stairs, and found Tucker in the same spot. "Radio the firefighters. Tell them Earl and Crispin are in the woods, unarmed as far as I can tell." She recounted what had just happened.

One of the teen girls gasped from the kitchen.

Tucker said, "Are you okay?"

Jayne nodded. *Lord, give me Your peace.*

He grasped the radio and relayed a warning to watch out for the two men.

"Camp," came the reply, all crackly. "Can you repeat that? You're breaking up. Wind…" The voice broke up. "…getting bad out here."

The connection went silent.

"Come in…" Tucker repeated his statement, asking the smokejumper crew to reply again.

When he got no answer, Jayne said, "I can head over there. I have gear and this gun." She didn't want to go out in the heat and wind wearing heavy gear, but she would in order to relay a message. "You all stay here and keep inside. Just in case."

"Yeah, I'm not gonna get far." He didn't look so happy about the fact his leg was broken, propped up on the couch.

"We need you coordinating. No one knows fire command here like you do." He wasn't exactly lying around doing nothing. She would probably be screaming in his position.

"Get me back in contact with them." He shifted in his seat and paled. Took a sip of the water glass on the table. "I'll text my wife again. Make sure all is good at home." He pointed to the table. "Take a radio. Stay in contact. Get them a message to decide if they want to come back here."

Jayne nodded. "Will do."

"The weather front is almost on top of us. I don't want anyone caught out in it if we can help it."

"I'll make sure they are safe and stay that way." She headed for the door. "You all know what to do if things turn hairy."

She headed out and jogged the trail to the fire road where they had gone. From their position they had two options: the lake or the camp. Neither was far.

She made it in ten minutes—a turnout coat on, a gun in one hand, and a radio in the other. By the time one of the smokejumpers spotted her, Jayne had sweat rolling down her back.

Someone peeled off and ran to her. She couldn't remember his name.

Orion raced over. Then Charlie. Alexis.

The other kids.

"What's going on?" Orion shoved by the smokejumper.

The smokejumper shoved him back. "The radio call from Tucker said Crispin and Earl? You saw them? They're here?"

"Okay, Booth," Orion said. "Back up. We need to make sure nothing else is going on." Orion eyed the gun in her hand.

"I'll hang on to that." Booth grabbed the gun and turned to look around. "Where did you see Earl and Crispin last?"

Who was this guy?

Jayne said, "Going north from the camp."

"They could come this way."

A female smokejumper stepped forward—the redhead. "*Could*. But the fire? It *is* coming."

"Tucker was trying to warn you to keep an eye out. But we should get out of this wind." Jayne watched the sky and the front coming in.

Charlie did the same.

She noted then that Alexis and Orion didn't seem so happy with him. What was going—

"There it goes." One of the boys whooped. "Fire tornado."

Jayne watched it twirl up into the sky. Lightning cracked to the east. The wind died enough that it quit blowing in her face.

Charlie took her hand, his fingers strong around hers.

Jayne said, "We need to get out of the open."

THIRTEEN

CHARLIE'S ENTIRE BODY SCREAMED AS HE TURNED. This was no time to have health problems. Especially not after what had happened with Orion and Alexis. Both of his children looked at him with disappointed expressions—something he never wanted. But then, it wasn't all that surprising, was it?

He'd never been someone the people who loved him could be proud of.

"Let's get back to the camp." Nova, one of the two female smokejumpers, took the lead.

They moved together as a group. Awareness swam around him with the buildup of heat in the air. It wasn't a good sign that the wind had dropped.

Jayne squeezed his hand. "Come on."

At least she hadn't asked him if he was all right.

Alexis glanced back, fear on her face. All the kids had banded together. Worry and fear hummed in the air like the heat as they ran down the trail, fire on both sides of them. He looked over his shoulder. "It's coming this way."

Jayne gasped. "That fire tornado keeps coming and it will pass over the camp." She lifted the radio.

"Tucker, come in." The unit crackled in her hand. She held it in front of her mouth, her knuckles a white grip on it. "Tucker, do you copy?"

"...read you." Tucker's voice sputtered. "...in the refrigerator."

"Be safe." Jayne said nothing else.

Nova glanced back. "What does the fridge mean?"

One of the teen boys said, "They're taking shelter in the walk-in fridge."

"Can we get back there?" Alexis asked.

Charlie said, "We have to try."

"That's not going to be possible." Logan, now up ahead, slowed. The group gathered around him. "The path is blocked."

Charlie spotted a tree over the path up ahead, the whole thing engulfed. They weren't going to be able to get back to camp.

Alexis spun to him. "What are we going to do?"

He motioned her over, and she slammed against him. Charlie spoke against her hair. "We're going to figure out a plan. All of us, together."

"We can go to the lake," one of the twins said.

The other stood beside him, nodding. "Drench ourselves in the water."

Before anyone could turn this into a debate, Charlie said, "Let's go."

Orion glanced at him, but then he and the teen boys ran ahead. Alexis and Jayne stuck with Charlie—at the back of the pack because he couldn't move that fast. How had he thought he could survive a whole season of firefighting and then end it all at the last minute?

He'd been an idiot. Pure and simple. God had made it plain that He had other ideas. He'd done an end-run around Charlie's plan and shown him everything he had to lose in just a few days.

You really want me to do this? I can't if we don't survive.

If God wanted him to be a father to his two kids and have the kind of relationship he'd always wanted with a woman, then He would have to keep them alive through this.

It was that simple.

Charlie was prepared to sit up and take notice where he'd always thought he didn't need God. But they had to get through this first.

He squeezed Jayne's hand. More of a reflex than anything. They were at the lake. He could slow to a walk with her, like they used to do, while the others looked at the fire raging around the lake.

"We could swim to the floating dock?" The twins and the smokejumpers, and Orion, debated back and forth.

Smoke filled the sky, like a storm of ash overhead.

Charlie turned and looked at the fire in the sky, racing toward them. "We won't be able to breathe when that gets here."

"Well, what are we going to do then?" Tears rolled down one of the twins' faces, and his brother hugged his neck. "We're going to die out here."

"You think I'm gonna let that happen?" Logan turned his back to Charlie, getting between him and the boys. "We're going to figure this out, okay? We didn't come this far to give up."

Jayne shifted to face him. Alexis gathered close.

Charlie looked at the lake, then the shed. "The boats." An idea coalesced in his mind. "We won't be able to breathe unless we make pockets of air. Unless we get in the water to keep ourselves from burning."

"What are you talking about?" Orion strode over.

There wasn't much time to explain. "Flip the boat, hang on. Use the air in the underside to keep us alive."

Nova said, "Are there enough—"

Orion already had the shed door open. "Guys! Help me with the boats. There should be enough for all of us."

Jayne said, "Split up evenly, campers and adults. I want everyone covered."

They hauled the boats to the water.

"It's hot." Alexis swiped at her face, then waded in, not saying anything else.

Charlie glanced at the fire arcing up to the sky. "Hurry." He waved over a couple of teens. The kid from Last Chance County, Izan's brother. "Come on."

It was their best shot if that fire passed over. The wind started to pick up again, ruffling his shirt against him. Sending Jayne's hair in front of her face so that she had to tuck wayward strands behind her ears.

The smokejumpers carried the boats out above their heads by twos or threes.

"Is this a good idea?"

Charlie didn't realize he'd spoken aloud until Orion squeezed his shoulder and said, "It's good thinking. It could be our best shot until this firestorm blows over."

"He's right." Jayne kissed his cheek. "I need to make sure the kids know who they're going with."

The smokejumpers were in up to their necks now but didn't seem to want to commit to going under a boat until they absolutely had to. They placed the boats on the water, holding on as the water bobbed the boats beside them like this was any day of lake recreation.

Help us, Lord.

Charlie waded in beside Alexis, who stood in the water up to her elbows. He gathered her to him in a hug again, needing it probably as much as she did.

Booth glanced over from beside a boat about ten feet away. "Afterwards, we need to talk about Crispin, okay?"

Charlie nodded.

Nova looked at Booth with a disappointed scowl. "We're about to die and you're worrying about some guy you've never met?"

"Never said I've never met him," Booth fired back.

"Well, then, who is he to you?"

They were really going to have an argument right now? Charlie sighed.

Booth said, "I could tell you, but then I'd have to kill you."

A couple of the teens let out nervous laughter. Good to ease the tension, but Charlie wasn't sure Booth was *entirely* joking.

Nova rolled her eyes. "Is this another one of your crazy stories?"

Before Booth could reply, Orion yelled, "Sparky!"

Everyone spun around to see the dog running toward them on the bank, his tail smoking, looking a little singed all over.

"Come here, boy!" Orion waded over and caught the dog up in his arms. "You're a good boy. Yes, you are."

The relief was palpable, even with the fire approaching.

The teens waded over to pet the dog.

"Reminds me of this story I heard," Booth began. "There's this military working dog, and he's trained to find dangerous chemicals. But he was in danger, right?" He paused to make sure the teens were listening.

Jayne glanced at Charlie, a relieved smile on her face. He waved her over, and she came to stand by his side in the water up to their waists.

Booth continued, "I have some friends who run this protection agency, and one of them was hired as a bodyguard. For the dog."

Nova snorted. "As if."

"Hey, that dog is a hero." Booth shot her a scathing look. "A national treasure."

She rolled her eyes. "Your stories are ridiculous. You really expect us to believe all that nonsense about CIA officers and stolen nukes? I saw that movie."

"Me too. And you know what?"

Nova waited.

"They lived happily ever after."

"Too bad it's not real."

Booth eyed her. "Yeah. Too bad."

Alexis shifted against Charlie's side. "It's getting closer. The air is getting hotter."

Jayne touched her shoulder. "No matter what, we don't let go of each other."

Orion looked over at the three of them in a huddle, something a lot like longing on his face. Missing what he'd never have. Charlie wanted to tell him to come over and stand with them, but the teen boys needed the man they knew well and the dog he'd adopted to keep them steady.

His son was the best kind of man. Because that

was what God had done in Orion's life—built character through trials. "I love all of you."

Orion nodded.

Jayne and Alexis both looked up at him. He kissed Alexis on the forehead then turned and kissed Jayne's cheek. Lingered.

"You guys can get a room. Later." Alexis made a face. "Right now we need to not die." She shot him a pointed look.

Charlie said, "You were right." She needed to know. "I don't plan on going anywhere."

"We need to get the boat over us." Jayne didn't want to look at the fire coming toward them. "The air is too hot."

Charlie let go of her and Alexis. He lowered himself under the water and came up soaking. "Everyone dunk yourselves and then get under the boats!"

One of the male smokejumpers said, "Why am I getting baptism vibes?"

The kids and firefighters all sank under the water one by one, getting their hair and clothes completely wet.

This is probably a terrible idea. But what else could they do?

Cold from the water greeted the hot air, and steam rose from everyone. "Orion?"

Her son glanced over. "I've got them." He nodded. "I'll see you on the flip side."

"I love you."

He mouthed, *Love you too.*

Orion and one of the other male smokejumpers flipped their boat, and four teen boys got under it. They walked out to where they wouldn't have to crouch—or tread water—and lowered so the edges of the boat touched the surface.

"If the wind picks up, we'll have to hang on. Hold the boats down." Logan looked at Charlie. "You guys good?"

Charlie nodded.

They pushed the boat out a little farther. Jayne could already feel heat radiating off the metal.

"What…" Alexis pointed at the shore.

Jayne spotted Crispin running toward them. About ten feet behind, Earl, with his long hair, raced after him.

"Get under the boats. Everyone!" Booth waded toward the shore.

Charlie and a couple of the smokejumpers got the boat flipped. Jayne motioned Alexis to go with her and ducked under the surface. She came up under the shelter of the boat, Charlie's daughter right beside her.

"I'm Finn."

Jayne told him her name. "Nice to meet you."

The guy grinned. "You good, kid?"

Alexis gripped the seat above her head. "Peachy. Just another day at the lake, right?"

The second smokejumper in there with them, a woman, said, "We used to come up here when I was a kid. Some kind of open day for the camp, so the locals could see it. I'm Hannah, by the way."

"Right," Jayne said. "We used to do those. We should do one of those again. Maybe at the end of the summer."

Finn said, "Good idea. We can celebrate being alive."

Charlie broke through the surface of the water.

"What's going on outside?" Jayne wanted to cling to him, but that would mean letting go of the boat. They had to hold it down, or the superheated air from outside would get in. How long was it going to last?

Once the heat and flames blew over them, would HQ be able to send in a helicopter to evacuate them?

Lord, please keep everyone safe.

She had no idea what was going on in the other boats. Part of her wanted to swim over and check.

Charlie said, "Crispin is good. He should be—"

Sophie's brother popped up, spitting water. He ran a hand down his face. "Booth is right behind me."

The smokejumper popped up. He looked around. "Hannah. Finn. We're gonna rotate, check everyone is good."

Hannah nodded. "Letting go."

Crispin and Booth grasped the seat on the underside of the boat. Hannah and Finn disappeared under the water. The rest of them spread out.

Jayne's arms shook, but she didn't let go. "What happened to Earl?" He'd been chasing Crispin. Were any of them going to tell her what actually just happened?

A hard expression crossed Crispin's face. "Earl won't be joining our rescue party."

Booth said nothing.

Alexis whimpered.

A second later, Logan popped up in the middle. He gasped a breath. "All good in here?"

Jayne said, "Is Orion okay?"

"He should be in here next. He traded with Nova

and Vince. They're telling the boys terrible jokes." Logan shook his head. "I'd have gone with bizarre facts no one would ever believe, but no one asked me." He disappeared under the surface.

Orion came up a second later.

"It's like Times Square in here," Booth said. "How's it going, kid?"

Orion glanced at him. Then he said, "You okay, Mom?"

"Yes, honey."

He turned to Charlie. "Dad?"

"I'm good, son."

A lump gathered in Jayne's throat. She refused to walk with the guilt of the past hanging over her head. That wasn't what God wanted from her. Now that they had met, they could spend the rest of their lives getting to know each other.

Orion said, "If you need a kidney, I'll be giving you one of mine if I'm compatible."

"Only if I'm not." Everyone looked at Alexis. "You're not going to die, Dad. We're not going to let you."

Jayne sniffed. It wasn't just water running down her face.

Charlie cleared his throat. "We'll see how it goes."

Crispin said, "I need to visit my sister."

"Houston is a good guy. The best, actually," Booth said. "She'll be okay until this is over and we find what we're looking for."

Jayne was too worried about what was going on outside and the people still at the camp to ask what that was about. *Your stories are ridiculous.* Nova's comment rolled through her mind.

Whatever was going on with Crispin seemed to

involve Booth somehow. And it was definitely above her pay grade.

The boat started to rock.

"I'm gonna check on the boys. You all hang on." Orion waited until Alexis nodded, then disappeared under the surface.

Booth and Crispin turned and started to whisper to each other. Alexis moved hand over hand along the boat toward the end where she was with Charlie.

Jayne shifted nearer to him, and the three of them hung there in a huddle, treading water and grasping the wood beam overhead.

"Is Orion going to be okay going out there?" Alexis bit her lip.

"He'll be good." Jayne wanted her son where she could see him but had to balance that with the fact that he was a grown man. One who cared deeply about others. "Until he goes ahead with wanting to be a smokejumper."

Charlie lifted one eyebrow.

"I know, I know. I'm determined to be okay with it." Jayne smiled. "At least to his face. When he's out, I'll be crying in my prayer closet until I know he's back at base."

If he insisted on putting his life in the hands of a parachute, he would have to deal with her worry. But she wasn't going to burden him with it.

She was going to take it to the Lord, the God who had always protected them.

Charlie smiled. "I'll probably be in there with you."

Because he wouldn't be out fighting fires? He'd be at home, fighting a different battle? She wanted to ask what he wanted. Maybe he hadn't figured it out.

Either way, God held their future in His hands.

"'For me, be it Christ, be it Christ hence to live,'" she said. "'If Jordan above me shall roll...'"

The boat rocked, tossed around by the wind.

They all held on tight. Even Booth and Crispin broke off their whispering to hold on in silence.

"'No pang shall be mine, for in death as in life...'" No matter what happened.

No matter how this ended.

She said, "'Thou wilt whisper Thy peace to my soul.'"

"Amen," Alexis said.

FOURTEEN

NOVA AND VINCE TUGGED ON THE BOAT, SO Charlie let go. They dragged it through the shallow water onto the beach. Charlie glanced around, getting a quick head count. "Everyone good?"

Some replied. Others looked over. Shell-shocked was an accurate assessment of their faces.

Every bit of brush and every tree he could see had been burned black.

The air seemed to crackle with energy, like he could touch a tree and it would fall to pieces. Destroyed.

They'd come so close to the end.

Thank You, Lord. They were safe.

Jayne spoke to each one of the teens individually. Making sure they were all right physically so they could work through the emotional and mental aspects now—and probably for the rest of their lives. Some of these kids would never let this day go. It would shape the adults they became.

"Dude, that was crazy." Samuel strode past, his brother Joshua in tow. Pablo glanced at Charlie.

The kid hesitated a second, then came over to Charlie with his hand out.

Charlie clasped it. "You guys good?"

All three boys nodded. Pablo said, "We're good." Cleared his throat and sniffed. Like all of them hadn't cried at least a little.

"It was pretty unbelievable for a while there, but it's over now," Charlie said. "First chance you get, call home. Tell them you're all right."

They wandered off.

"I'm all right." Alexis appeared by his side, burrowing in again. "Just in case you were curious."

"Always."

"You need a doctor to look at you."

Charlie figured there was zero chance he'd get out of that. Probably no point in arguing with her, or Orion. Or Jayne. Or anyone else. He didn't even bother cataloguing how he felt. He just needed a good spot to lie down and close his eyes.

They were alive.

Jayne gave Tiger a hug and headed toward the group starting toward the camp trail. Alexis held Charlie's hand as they walked.

"You're really going to do this?" Alexis glanced over, walking his pace, and not in a way that let him know she was purposely slow just because of him. "You're going to fight this illness and do everything you can to live as long as possible."

Thou wilt whisper Thy peace to my soul.

He swallowed against the lump in his throat and nodded. "I will if you will."

Charlie still wasn't sure he'd ever be okay with one of them giving him a kidney. If he could do this without needing a transplant, that would be the best course. He might have to endure more that way, but it would be worth it, knowing he wasn't impeding their futures for his.

Alexis rolled her eyes. "You're such a dad."

He grinned, warm not just because of the lingering heat but also because he hadn't had many chances to feel that way. Or to prove that he could be the man he wanted to be.

Now he just needed to get Jayne to agree to let him try, and not just with his kids.

But with her.

Booth, Finn, and Vince had crowded around something on the shore. Charlie and Alexis got close enough, and he saw it was a burned body. Earl?

No one would cry over the death of an evil man. But a life had still been lost—and someone, somewhere, had cared about him.

Charlie steered Alexis away from the scene, but as they passed, he said to Booth, "Where did Crispin go?"

Booth glanced at Nova, then looked over. "We don't need to worry about Crispin."

Okay, then.

Jayne joined them. Alexis said, "Do you ever get used to seeing dead bodies like that?"

Charlie squeezed her with his arm and wrapped the other around Jayne so they could walk together down the scorched path to the camp. He prayed no one taking shelter there had been killed. "Not really. I don't think you ever get used to it. But you learn how to celebrate the time you have."

Time God had given them.

"I won't shed a tear," Jayne said. "He nearly killed us all. Land mines, and hurting Crispin? Setting fires and holding a gun to my head? Who cares what he wanted. He won't get it now."

Charlie shuddered. "We very nearly didn't make it."

The camp came into view.

Even the ground looked scorched. Paint had peeled off siding. A couple of windows were broken, and debris from what looked like one of the sheds was littered in pieces down the main street.

Teenage girls raced out of the main house, followed by smokejumpers carrying Tucker down the porch steps.

Alexis broke off to meet them, and there were a lot of relieved hugs.

Charlie turned Jayne to face him, their bodies flush against each other.

"Charlie Benning." She shook her head. "So forward. What will our parents think?"

He felt a smile pull up the edge of his mouth. Before he could reply to her, the sound of a helicopter crested the hill.

Two helicopters.

He kept Jayne close with one arm and used the other to shield his eyes.

The first chopper to land was the local medical emergency transport. The other was pure black, and the men who hopped out were dressed in tactical gear.

Aria broke off from her friends. "Dad!" She raced to the men.

The blond spotted Charlie and lifted two fingers. Charlie returned the gesture. Aria slammed into the man with Asian heritage. The others gathered around her.

Jayne said, "Friends of yours?"

Charlie looked at Jayne.

"I feel like I'm missing something," she said. "I know who Aria's family is, but should I know those guys aside from what I've read?"

"They might have come here to check on Aria and make sure she's okay, but they will also help get the rest of us out of here. They're good people." Helping the innocent was what the men of Chevalier Protection Specialists did.

"She's fortunate to have them in her life, then."

Charlie nodded. "Yes, she is."

The other smokejumpers helped Tucker to the medical chopper, and Bridget walked with them. Everyone had come through. Not unscathed, but not far from it.

"Looks like we're leaving."

Charlie said, "There's just one thing I need to do before we go."

She gave him a knowing look. "And what's that?"

He turned and dipped her. Pressed his lips to hers and tried to find some of that magic they'd had between them before. It crackled at the edges in a way that had nothing to do with the air pressure or the fire.

Then the spark hit him full force, a wave of heat. The storm of everything they'd once had, layered with a whole lot of maturity. Life lived in the interim years.

Everything they'd been through and learned.

She clung to his neck, and they rediscovered what would always be between them.

All the while, several people cheered. Clapped.

Someone whooped. Charlie tuned it all out. Then he stood up, bringing her with him. Loving the flush on her cheeks. "What do you say? Want to ride in a chopper with me?"

She grinned. "I thought you'd never ask."

A NOTE FROM LISA

Dear Reader,

The second I found out my book was called *Firestorm*, I just knew I had to include one in the story! You know I love my explosions, and crazy shenanigans plots, but the chance to set the sky on fire? Oh yes, count me in for that—and packing in as many character cameos as I could.

Writing a series that's the intersection of Susan May Warren's story universe and the Last Chance County/Benson world was the most exciting thing I could've dreamed of. It's been an adventure since I first approached Sunrise Publishing about being a lead author, and this series is everything I wanted out of jumping on board with Susie and the whole Sunrise family.

I'm excited for everything we have coming soon, like the EPIC conclusion to this series. And in the future, with more Last Chance Fire and Rescue books, more epic romantic suspense (Logan and Jamie, anyone??) and so many more plans I can't even tell you about. Yet. If you love great books, be sure to subscribe to the Sunrise newsletter so you find out as soon as they're available.

Firestorm was a party and a half, pure fun, and a pleasure to write. The whole series is epic, but these characters just crawled into my heart and decided who they were going to be. Who knew Charlie had a life, a daughter, a past he never told us about, and a son he didn't know he had? God certainly surprised him when Charlie set out on a summer that was supposed to be his last. He planned to go out of this world on his terms, but God had a future for him.

Isn't that how it goes?

We think we know how things will play out, or we make plans. God has better ones! Charlie went from a man with no future to a blessed guy with the woman he loved in his life, two great kids, and the will to take a shot at survival. Because he had a reason to live.

If you or someone you know is struggling to find a reason to live, please reach out to your local suicide hotline. There's no shame in asking for help, and no reason to wait.

God numbers our days, and He walks each step alongside us. He is our peace, our hope. I know He holds you in His hands and will draw near to you as you draw near to Him.

I'm praying for you.

Firestorm had a thread from a famous hymn in it. Did you notice that through the series so far? I love old hymns, and when Susie suggested we include the stanzas as our spiritual thread for each of the stories I agreed it was a great idea.

Mine was:

For me, be it Christ, be it Christ hence to live: If Jordan above me shall roll, No pang shall be mine, for in death as in life Thou wilt whisper Thy peace to my soul. It is well, with my soul, It is well, it is well with my soul.

Jayne had to find that peace as much as Charlie. She had her own road to travel, and leaned on God to bring her to the life He had waiting for her.

I'm praying that God whispers His peace to your soul.

I have to say a huge thank you to my amazing reader community on Discord. Each of you is a dear friend. I enjoy chatting with you, swapping prayer requests and recipes, talking about great books, and supporting each other. Thank you so much for making this author thing not feel so solitary.

Thanks to Megan, Michelle, and Kate for contending with the edits and revisions I threw at you through this process. I learn so much with each series and continue to grow as a mentor and editor. It was a pleasure seeing these great ideas come to life as amazing books.

Until next time, friends.

Happy Reading,

Lisa

Thank you for reading *Firestorm*! Gear up for the next Chasing Fire: Montana romantic suspense thriller, *Fireline* by Kate Angelo. Keep reading for a sneak peek!

SECRETS. BETRAYAL. SACRIFICE.
THIS TIME, THEY'RE NOT JUST
FIGHTING FIRE.

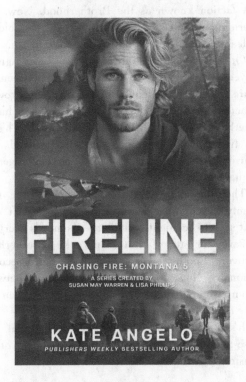

She was born to be a smokejumper...

As the niece of a legendary smokejumper, Nova Burns is tough as nails. When their crew chief Tucker

Newman breaks his leg, Nova longs for the opportunity to helm the team, ready to take risks and prove herself. But there's one risk she refuses to take — falling in love.

He's living a lie...

Undercover Homeland agent Booth Wilder is seeking redemption. Scarred by a past explosion that took the life of his partner, Booth is hunting a rogue CIA faction known as the Brotherhood. Now, he's determined to uncover their secrets and find a hidden nuclear weapon that could turn the world to ash.

Only problem...summer sparks have ignited between Booth and Nova. Nova is torn between her future as the smokejumping chief, her growing attraction to Booth, and the belief that he's hiding something from her. Of course he is...Booth is hiding his true goal — unrooting the Brotherhood and returning to his life as a Homeland Security agent, a life that he's not sure he really wants.

Then the wildfire threatens the home of the Jude County Firefighting team, and Nova doesn't care what secrets he might be hiding — she needs everyone to save the town. But when the Brotherhood discovers Booth and his goals, the fight becomes personal. Now, Booth must choose between accomplishing his mission and saving the woman he's come to love.

It's a dangerous game of loyalty, betrayal, and pulse-pounding action in the fifth installment of the Chasing Fire: Montana series.

FIRELINE

CHASING FIRE: MONTANA | BOOK 5

CHAPTER 1

His enemies had found him.

All this time and they'd come so far. They'd nearly finished it.

Now it would all be for nothing.

The plane dropped about a hundred feet somewhere over the Kootenai National Forest. Okay, maybe it was fifty. Twenty. Booth Wilder didn't know. Turbulence mixed with dread and exhilaration of what he was about to do left him nauseated.

The six-man crew of smokejumpers was packed in tight. Shoulder to shoulder. All crowded around the windows according to their jump order.

Booth sat with Nova Burns, a thrill-seeking legacy smokejumper with a propensity toward bossiness. Behind them were Finn and Vince, the two sawyers who'd be out front clearing the brush for the crew. Last in line was Logan, the team lead, and JoJo, another seasoned smokejumper.

He glanced at the stoic faces. These jumpers, they had families, homes, lives outside the smoke. Booth wasn't even sure who he was anymore. Just a WITSEC nobody. No past, no future, just this endless free fall until Homeland gave him back his life.

"You good?" Nova shouted into the side of his helmet.

"Better if Aria didn't plow through every air pocket like she was flyin' an F-22," he yelled over the roar of the engines. "I miss Tirzah!"

"Whatever. Aria is every bit a daredevil pilot. We were lucky to get her from Alaska!" She shouted into her headphone mic, "Hey, Aria! Ever think of becoming a fighter pilot?"

"Why you think I carry a .357 Magnum?" Her voice crackled over the intercom. "I just stick my arm out the window and pew pew pew."

Laughter filled the fuselage but cut off when the plane hit another patch of turbulence. They slammed down on the cargo. The mirth turned to grumbling.

Vince rubbed his elbow. "For real. If Aria doesn't take it easy, I'll have to jump outta this plane."

"Please tell me someone packed Huggies in the cargo box for Vince." Their spotter for the day, Eric Dale, laughed over the intercom.

Booth peered out the window. The charred remains of the mountain landscape rushed past at a hundred miles an hour. Thousands of lush green acres lay blackened, ravaged by the wildfire. To the west, black veins of ash pulsed through a crimson expanse.

Somewhere out there in the endless wilderness was the real Crazy Henry from the stories Booth told by the fire.

And Crispin.

Three years since the nuke had gone missing.

Three years since his life had fallen apart.

They'd said his former partner was dead. So why was Crispin here, in Ember of all places?

Was his appearance connected to Earl's death? Was this where the nuke trail led? If Crispin was playing some deep game, Booth needed to see the board. Maybe finding him would lead him to the nuke, and maybe it would lead him back to himself.

He had to find Crispin. That was the goal. But how? This town was a haystack, and he was searching for the needle blindfolded.

The plane bounced and fell again. Queasiness sloshed around his stomach. His breathing was tight, restricted by the straps on his jump harness. He'd never been so eager to jump from a plane before.

"Still good?" Nova nudged his knee.

"Fine. Just...thinking."

The plane winged down into a hard turn. They turned their attention back to the windows as the plane circled the fire, giving them a closer look. Two hundred acres of fierce flames shot out from the trees, sending billows of dense black smoke spiraling into the sky. Booth's chest constricted. The fire raged in every direction.

Eric left his seat from the cockpit and picked his way through the tangle of jumpers. At the door, he attached the restraining line to his harness so that if he fell out, they could pull him back in. Booth had seen it happen once, so he'd never forget the restraining line.

"Guard your reserves!" Eric yelled.

Booth and every other jumper covered their reserve chute with a forearm to protect it from accidental deployment when the door opened. Booth had seen that happen too.

Eric grabbed the handles and twisted. The door hinged back toward the tail of the plane. Cold air and the scent of woodsmoke rushed in.

Nova stood at the jump doors, face hidden behind the wire-mesh guard on her helmet. "Fire's about twenty-five miles northeast of Snowhaven. Wind conditions aren't much better than yesterday, and the head is pushing southwest toward an area with a few homesteads."

"They've called for evacuations," Logan said. "But we know not everyone takes it seriously."

"Yeah, there's always one who thinks they can ride it out," Finn said.

"Buddy check," Nova said, pulling on her fire gloves. "Booth's with me first stick. Logan and Vince, second stick. JoJo and Finn, third."

Booth went to the door and performed his four-point check.

Nova stuck her head out of the plane beside Eric. Booth watched over Nova's shoulder as Eric dropped the first set of drift streamers. They watched them fall. The long pieces of weighted crepe paper fell toward the ground, catching on currents.

Booth did some quick mental calculations and determined wind drift and descent time. "Looks good?"

Eric nodded his agreement. "Aria, take us to three thousand!"

Aria's voice crackled over the intercom. "We're at three thousand."

"All right. Looks like about a hundred fifty yards of drift. The wind is strongest down low. Stay wide of the fire." Eric's head swung out the opening, then he turned back. "Get in the door!"

Booth backed up to give Nova room. She sat on the floor and braced herself. Her feet dangled out into the slipstream, ready to jump into the vast canvas of the sky. He dropped into position and moved in tight behind her. The hum of the plane vibrated under his legs. Nova leaned back. Pressed herself into his chest.

The familiar tingle of raw energy electrified his muscles. Nerves firing. Blood pumping. Countless jumps and he couldn't shake the mix of fear and exhilaration seconds before the free fall. He took a deep breath. The crisp air filled his lungs. This was it. The moment before the plunge.

Eric's slap came down on Nova's shoulder, and she propelled herself forward out into the wind.

Booth rocked forward as hard as he could to miss the edge of the door but bumped it on the way out. He tumbled under the tail of the plane in a slow spin and turned his belly to the ground.

The rush of wind, the weightlessness, and the deafening roar of the air enveloped him. In that moment, all fear and doubt were left behind. His past mistakes were replaced by the freedom of flight. He had nothing but the sky and the guilt of surviving when others hadn't.

He counted in his head and kept his eyes on the horizon. "Jump thousand…look thousand…reach thousand…wait thousand…"

Once stable, he pulled the rip cord. "Pull thousand!"

A hard jerk pulled at his chest straps. The parachute riffled open high above the burning landscape. For a moment there was nothing but Booth, the wind in his ears, and the land below. Nothing but him and the God who had spoken all this into being. The wildfire ravaged the divine canvas, but underneath it all, there was a promise of renewal and rebirth.

This was the part he loved. He'd come to Ember looking for a place to lay low, but jumping had gotten into his blood. But did he love it enough if the time came for him to choose between this life and the dead one?

He grabbed the steering toggles and turned to face the hundreds of miles of wilderness. Smoke rose high overhead, gathering in storm clouds. Violent flames whipped back and forth between the trees.

Nova was right. This thing had the potential to go big. The other crews needed all the help they could get. They needed him.

Booth descended through open sky. The only audible sounds were the distant hum of the jump ship and the gentle flutter of his parachute as he glided twenty-five hundred feet above the earth.

"Oooooh-weeeee!" Nova yelled.

Booth grinned and let out his own whooping shout.

Between his feet, wind whipped Nova's chute to the west. She swept over a dense stand of towering Douglas firs. He caught the same wind gust and steered hard, but the wind pulled him toward the same trees.

Facing into the wind, he tried to locate the jump spot through the thick smoke.

The chute rocked back and forth. Booth's gut tightened.

He pulled down on the left toggle and moved closer to the wind line. The strong smell of smoke filled the air and stung his nostrils.

Two hundred feet to go and he could barely see the ground through the dense ash cloud. "I can't see the spot!"

"It's gonna be a hanger!" Nova hollered something else he couldn't hear.

Another headwind blew him backward and into the woods. This was turning out to be more dangerous than catching bad guys. Forget making the spot. He just needed to land somewhere without hanging up.

At a hundred feet, things got worse. The wind died and he moved forward, but it was too late to clear the trees. He entered the opening at treetop level just in time to see Nova crash into a thick stand of birch and disappear.

Barely missing some of the taller trees, he reefed down on his left toggle and flew between two towering trunks. His canopy brushed trees, tearing and snagging on smaller branches as he passed. Instead of slowing down, he began to speed up in a free fall.

The ground was steep, and he teetered on the edge of slamming into it. All this time doing the right thing, biding his time, holding himself apart from the world, for it to end like this.

And there was nothing he could do about it.

Nova's parachute billowed above her, snagging branches on the way down. The world became a blur of green and brown, branches whipping past. Her boot clipped a tree branch. The choked scream died in her throat.

This was it. Her legacy. Another smiling portrait on the memorial wall back at jump base.

The thick fabric caught and sent a jolt running through her body as she jerked to a stop. She swung back and forth, suspended six feet above the unforgiving earth.

Six feet. Six feet from being another memory for someone. Six feet from another empty space at the dinner table.

Nova closed her eyes and blew out a tight breath. That was ridiculous. "You're a smokejumper, Nova. This is what you do. You survive."

But what if *they* didn't?

Nerves had her hands shaking as she put the drogue release in her pocket. "Booth, am I safe to let down?" She looked around but didn't see him.

"Booth?"

Overhead, tree limbs rustled. Booth plummeted down between two big birch trees, grunting and growling all the way down. Branches ripped at his jump gear and tore his chute.

"Booth!"

Calling his name was dumb. All she could do was hang there and watch him fall end over end through the trees and pray his gear did its job.

His arms and legs snagged branches, broke loose, and he got hung up again. The chute caught a limb and jerked him over. He landed head down between two branches, suspended inches off the ground.

He swung there for a second, then laughed. "At least I didn't hit the—"

A branch cracked. The chute pulled loose. Booth came crashing down into the underbrush and hit the ground. A second later he rolled to his back and groaned.

Nova winced. "Ouch. Are you okay?"

Booth's thumb shot up.

"Hang on, I'm coming down." Nova found her letdown tape in a leg pocket and threaded it between the V formed by her riser. "Inside, outside. Outside, inside."

The chant helped her remember to route the tape over the top of the main letdown line and secure herself to the riser. She tied off using three half hitches and ran the rest of the tape. She did the five-point check and released the risers.

She eased down, letting the tape slide through her gloved hands in a smooth descent. Her boots hit the forest floor, and she pulled her helmet off.

Nova ran to Booth and leaned over him. "Seriously, are you hurt? That looked painful."

"Wow. I didn't know you cared." Booth got to his feet and pulled his helmet off to reveal a toothy smile. He tossed his disheveled hair. "Good jump, huh?"

"Good jump? We could've broken our necks."

"Hey, anything I walk away from is a good jump in my book." The shadow of something unspoken passed over his eyes. "I'm just glad we're both safe."

"Yeah, me too."

Nova called the plane and let them know their status. "Visibility is shot with all this smoke. And the wind gusts are a bit worse than we thought. Remind the crew of letdown procedures, because they'll probably get treed up."

"Ten-four," Eric said. "The rest of the crew is coming down in a new jump spot with better visibility." He gave her the coordinates and she confirmed.

Nova checked the navigation. Two paths looked promising.

She grabbed her helmet and secured it to her pack. "Ridge. It's quicker."

"Hold on, Wildfire Girl." Booth dusted himself off. "That's a steep, rocky climb and closer to the fire. We could get cut off. Let's take the forest."

"It's too dense. We'll spend hours cutting through the underbrush."

"It's safer than us being trapped like sitting ducks," Booth said, packing his chute with a bit more force than needed.

Why was he always so stubborn? "Look, the fire won't wait. Your route will take twice as long, and that's precious time we don't have. We're taking the ridge. Grab your gear and let's go."

"Fine." Booth nodded, a flicker of something unreadable in his eyes. He hoisted his pack and set off.

As she followed Booth on the rocky trail, Nova couldn't shake the feeling that her voice, her decision, was lost in the smoke. It'd be nice if maybe, just once, Booth would listen to her instead of looking at her like she was a loose cannon waiting to explode.

It wasn't like this was her first rodeo. Following in her uncle Jock's footsteps, she'd joined the hotshot crew in high school and dug an uphill line for three years, followed by three more on the helitack crew before she'd made smokejumper. Booth had only... wait, she wasn't even sure of his history.

That man was nothing but a mystery sometimes.

They hiked the ridgeline for about six miles,

keeping a hard eye on the fire. The entire time, Nova ran fire entrapment training videos through her mind. If the fire started to overrun them, she had two or three escape routes planned.

They found the clearing about an hour later. Nova dropped her spent chute and her gear. She took an assessing glance at her team. All but one cargo drop had been unloaded, but by the looks of it, Vince, JoJo, and Finn would have it done in no time.

Logan carried a box of water on his shoulder, looking like the perfect hero some people seemed to think he was. He set the box down and grinned. "Glad you could join us."

"Gnarly landing, and a bit of a hike here, but we're in one piece." Nova flicked a glance at Booth, but he didn't chime in. "How 'bout you guys?"

"Came down with far less flair." Logan waved a hand at the boxes. "We've got the gear inventoried, and we're about to pack what we need for this trip."

"We got a firsthand look at the fire coming down," Nova said. "We've got a steep slope, so we can start in with a direct saw line at the tail and work up. Redirect the fire north." She clapped her hands. "Let's pack up and head out, ASAP."

In under an hour, they had all their gear to the tail of the fire. It was midafternoon, and if Nova was sweating, the rest of them were probably drenched. "Grab some water before we put together a strategy."

Nova drank from her canteen and studied the fire that burned some fifty feet away, beyond a meadow where the smokejumpers had already cut a wide line. From here she was safe, but the heat was intense, even with the distance.

"Okay, team, looks like the fire is a little over two

acres. Totally doable if the wind doesn't push us." She slid the map from her pocket and laid it on the ground. "Right in this area, there are two homesteads in the path of the fire. First priority is to save any locals who didn't evac."

"There's another house way out here." Logan tapped the map northeast. "The fire's pretty far and pushing south, so shouldn't be a problem."

Nova nodded. "Good. Once we get the line cut here, Logan, take JoJo and go up the right flank. Booth, Vince, and Finn hit the left. I'll scout up to the head of the fire and check the homesteads."

"I think it's better if I go with you," Booth said. "It's safer if we stay in pairs, and I can help once we get to the head."

Had Booth ever taken a single order without second-guessing her? "I can handle myself—"

"He's got a point," Logan said. "This is basically one big spot fire. We can handle it, can't we?" JoJo, Vince, and Finn voiced their agreement in unison.

She clenched her teeth and bit back the snarky comment threatening to fly out. Logan took Booth's side and encouraged the rest of the team to do the same. He might be aiming to beat her out as new crew chief, but she was team lead for this fire.

She looked at Booth. "I guess if the team can manage without you, then you're with me."

Logan clapped his gloved hands together. "Okay, let's secure this tail!"

Flames leaped up from the trees lining the southern perimeter. Billowing columns of dense black smoke rolled through the air, dimming the sun to a dull red. Crackles and hisses emanated from the dead trees and fallen logs.

Nova keyed the radio to contact commander Miles Dafoe to check on the air attack. They could use a water drop.

Vince sized up a birch tree for about twenty seconds. He cranked up his chainsaw and dogged in. The man was a magician with a saw. And with a father as a captain in Cal Fire, fire had probably been his whole life like it had been for Nova.

Finn, the youngest on the team, went to work cutting out the brush and downed logs. The rest of the crew started in with their Pulaskis, scraping away the forest litter down to mineral soil to make a barrier that would be hard for the fire to cross.

An hour later, Nova and Booth weren't far from the first homestead when she heard a plane rumbling in the sky.

Her radio crackled. "Burns, we're coming up on your area. Clear for drop?"

She checked with Logan, and he confirmed they were all outside the drop zone. "Ten-four, tanker. We're clear for drop."

"Copy."

The plane rumbled in low. Overhead, there was a brilliant flash, and the air filled with rain. The water came down over the forest behind them.

"Let's move," Nova said to Booth. "The wind is pushing the fire fast. I'd like to get to those homesteads before it does." Their best hope was to get to the houses and make sure the owners had evacuated.

She trailed behind Booth, stepping over rocks and branches and using her Pulaski as a walking stick. They kept roughly a hundred yards from the fire. Enough so they could keep an eye on it, but still close enough to feel the heat on the side of her face.

They walked maybe a mile through dense forest. The fire had slowed with the water drop. The air was not quite as smoky when they arrived at the narrow dirt driveway.

"There it is." She jogged past Booth to a small cabin with a lean-to porch and knocked on the door. "Anyone home?"

Booth cupped his hands and pressed his face to the window. "It's empty."

"You sure?"

"Yeah. Looks like a one-room hunting cabin." He pointed to an upright wooden rectangle over to the right of the cabin with a moon carved into the door. "Outhouse."

"Huh. Must be a hotshot, or someone who knows about wildland firefighting." Nova nodded to the twelve-inch-wide trench encircling the property.

"That's some fire line," Booth said. "How far to the next?"

"Half mile. Hydrate and let's go."

Booth struck out ahead, his long legs making the hustle easier for him. "You really think anyone's there?"

"You'd be surprised." She tried not to huff and puff with the heat and the exertion. "People are crazy about protecting their property."

He stepped over a fallen tree blocking the path. "That sounds like personal experience talking."

Nova's heart stuttered a beat. It was personal experience talking, wasn't it?

Her parents had refused to abandon their livelihood to a wildfire and died trying to save it. Even though it'd meant leaving her behind. They'd chosen the homestead over her. "Everyone finds their worth in something. Homes, jobs, kids, relationships. Sometimes it's to their own detriment."

He shot a glance over his shoulder.

She squinted. "What's that look for?"

"Nothing. I mean, you're right." He skirted a boulder and used a tree limb to steady himself. "No one would stay up in these mountains without a really good reason."

"People go into the wilderness to find solitude and serenity." As if anyone ever could. Not completely.

"I heard you grew up on a homestead in the mountains. Did you find tranquility here?"

"No."

Booth stopped and turned to face her. "Boy, you sure don't open up easily."

Nova took a long pull on her water and recapped the canteen. "Neither do you."

Their eyes locked. It seemed they both held unspoken truths they dared not utter.

Stalemate.

She marched past Booth. "We're almost there. Let's keep moving."

Ten minutes later they broke through the forest to the homestead, both now breathing hard.

"Oh no." Nova pushed to a run. God, don't let there be anyone inside.

The fire had beaten them here.

Twenty yards ahead, the flames roared through the underbrush, sizzling, cracking, and popping. Orange flames shot up forty to fifty feet on either side of a quaint structure and whipped through the treetops over the metal roof.

Showers of embers rained down. Sparks blew upward and lodged in the branches of a thick black spruce beside the cabin.

She grabbed her radio and called the command desk as she ran up the porch steps. "The head is fanning out at the second homestead. We need a tanker."

"Copy that. Anybody home up there?"

"Checking. We'll save any civilians. Just get that mud up here so we can slow this fire down." She banged on the door. "Hey! Anyone in there? Jude County Smokejumpers! Open up!"

Voices. Footsteps pounded the floor. The doorknob rattled. A bearded man opened the door. He had a muscled arm wrapped around a woman. Probably his wife.

For a second, Nova stared at the couple, so similar to her own parents fifteen years ago. Parents who'd lived in a remote cabin in the mountains. Who'd poured their blood, sweat, and tears into a self-sustaining homestead.

The dirt and ash turned to mud in her mouth, and she swallowed it down. "Get out of the house."

"It's not a house. It's our home." The man lifted his chin. "Tell us what to do so we can save it."

Nova pushed away images from the past. "The fire is moving through here faster than we can keep up. We're doing what we can to contain it, but it's not safe for you to stay. You have to leave. That tree—didn't you get the evacuation notice?"

Stubborn people put their lives at risk thinking they could withstand a fire. And now their obstinacy might get her and Booth killed right along with them. This was her past repeating itself all over the place.

"We were out riding ATVs all morning. Smelled the smoke and headed back."

"If you had an escape, you should've taken it." Nova's words sounded cold. She shifted her weight and tried again. "Look, we need you to evac while you still can. It's worse than you realize."

The man opened the door wider and gaped at the flames consuming the forest less than fifty yards away. "It's…everywhere."

His wife squeezed his arm. "What're we gonna do?"

"I'm Daniel, and this is my wife, Teresa. We don't want to lose our home." He wrung his dry, calloused hands together. "Please tell us what to do."

Daniel's eyes held the same look her father's had when they'd faced the fire. This man might not be a fireman, but he was a hard worker. Like her father had been.

She hadn't been able to save them, but she could help save these people. "You got a chainsaw?"

A few minutes later, Teresa had a hose connected to the well water spigot and was drenching the ground in a line around the home. Daniel used his chainsaw to clear the brush while Booth worked to fell the thick spruce trees threatening to fall on the house.

Nova shoveled mounds of fresh dirt over the spot fires popping up. They were making progress digging a protective line around the property. If things went sideways, they'd run for the small pond on the back side of Daniel's property.

Booth cut the engine on the saw and wiped his brow. His face was black with sweat and grime. "This little chain saw can't cut this thick one fast enough. I shoulda been through it by now."

Nova's radio crackled. "Nova, we're five minutes to drop. We've got retardant. Clear the area."

"Copy." She wiped two dirty fingers on her shirt and popped them in her mouth. The shrill whistle caught everyone's attention. "Move to the porch! We've got incoming!"

Mud rained down on the roof and filled the air with a salty smell that reminded her of the ocean. The fire-retardant chemicals coated the forest, the grass, and the brush. The humidity level skyrocketed and the air cooled.

Teresa gasped.

Nova glanced at the woman. "It's pretty amazing, right?"

Beyond the older couple, Booth had his eyes on her, not the retardant drop. The darkness from his expression was gone now.

"You're missing the show."

A smile shone in his eyes. "No, I'm not."

She looked at the mess of foam, burnt grass, singed trees, and smoke all around them. So, pretty much her life.

Nothing but disaster and destruction.

Enough of that.

The retardant drop had knocked the flames down and cooled the running fire, but there was still work to do.

She hopped off the porch. "Back to work. Booth and I have a job to do."

Daniel followed. "You need an extra pair of hands?"

The homesteader worked hard, but Nova waffled.

"This is dangerous work. Besides the fire, we're constantly at risk of falling limbs. I think you'd better stay here and make that fire line wider. Now that the forest has burned, you won't have much fuel for another wildfire, but you should always be prepared."

"It'd be wise to take a few of the free classes the hotshot crew offers to learn how to protect your home," Booth said.

Teresa hugged Nova. "Thank you. We're so glad you got here when you did."

Nova stood rigid. It was just too weird to be hugged by someone who reminded her of her dead mother.

She let Teresa hold her a beat, then pulled away. "Just, uh, doing our jobs."

Booth and Nova worked all night to pinch off the head, and by early morning, Logan, Vince, Finn, and JoJo had connected the left and right flank lines. They'd contained the fire enough to stop its spread.

Thick gray clouds hovered in the early morning sky and blocked the sunrise. The team had their gear packed and stood in a line waiting.

"You did great work today." Nova scanned the soot- and dirt-covered faces of her crew. "You saved a family. I have new orders from Miles. We're going to split the team. Logan, JoJo, and Vince are gonna meet up with the rest of the Missoula crew working the main fire. My team has twenty-four-hour leave for rest and resupply."

"You heard her." Logan threw his arm forward. "Let's march."

Nova hefted her pack and followed Booth and Finn toward the clearing where they'd meet the chopper.

Today they'd saved a homestead from a fire not unlike the one that'd killed her parents. But Daniel and Teresa were safe, and Nova could live with that.

The danger wasn't over, though.

Not by far.

Beyond the charred remains of the contained fire, the air thrummed with the distant roar of the real beast. A two-thousand-acre inferno headed west, hungry for the town of Snowhaven.

ACKNOWLEDGMENTS

Huge thanks to my Sunrise family. Love working
with you all on such fun projects.
Let's keep the fires burning!

Looking for more more exciting romantic suspense from Sunrise Publishing?

DON'T MISS ANY CHASING FIRE: MONTANA STORIES

SECRETS. BETRAYAL. SACRIFICE.
THIS TIME, THEY'RE NOT JUST FIGHTING FIRE.

With heart-pounding excitement, gripping suspense, and sizzling (but clean!) romance, the CHASING FIRE: MONTANA series, brought to you by the incredible authors of Sunrise Publishing, including the dynamic duo of bestselling authors Susan May Warren and Lisa Phillips, is your epic summer binge read.

Immerse yourself in a world of short, captivating novels that are designed to be devoured in one sitting. Each book is a standalone masterpiece, (no story cliffhangers!) although you'll be craving the next one in the series!

Follow the Montana Hotshots and Smokejumpers as they chase a wildfire through northwest Montana. The pages ignite with clean romance and high-stakes danger—these heroes (and heroines!) will capture your heart. The biggest question is…who will be your summer book boyfriend?

DISCOVER OUR LAST CHANCE FIRE AND RESCUE SERIES

FIRE. FAMILY. FAITH.
LAST CHANCE FIRE AND RESCUE

Dive into this thrilling first responder series now!

FIND THEM ALL AT SUNRISE PUBLISHING!

AND DON'T MISS READING WHERE IT ALL BEGAN...

Read the origin stories of the Jude County Smokejumpers in Susan May Warren's Montana Fire series, kicking off with Jed Ransom's story in *Where There's Smoke*.

Grab the complete 9 book Montana Fire series now!

CONNECT WITH SUNRISE

Thank you again for reading *Firestorm*. We hope you enjoyed the story. If you did, would you be willing to do us a favor and leave a review? It doesn't have to be long—just a few words to help other readers know what they're getting. (But no spoilers! We don't want to wreck the fun!) Thank you again for reading!

We'd love to hear from you—not only about this story, but about any characters or stories you'd like to read in the future. Contact us at www.sunrisepublishing.com/contact.

We also have a monthly update that contains sneak peeks, reviews, upcoming releases, and fun stuff for our reader friends. Sign up at www.sunrisepublishing.com or scan our QR code.

ABOUT LISA PHILLIPS

Lisa Phillips is a USA Today and top ten Publishers Weekly bestselling author of over 80 books that span Harlequin's Love Inspired Suspense line, independently published series romantic suspense, and thriller novels. She's discovered a penchant for high-stakes stories of mayhem and disaster where you can find made-for-each-other love that always ends in happily ever after.

Lisa is a British ex-pat who grew up an hour outside of London and attended Calvary Chapel Bible College, where she met her husband. He's from California, but nobody's perfect. It wasn't until her

Bible College graduation that she figured out she was a writer (someone told her). As a worship leader for Calvary Chapel churches in her local area, Lisa has discovered a love for mentoring new ministry members and youth worship musicians.

Find out more at www.authorlisaphillips.com